MISTER B'S
LAND

Other Books by LaJoyce Martin:

The Harris Family Saga:
To Love a Bent-Winged Angel
Love's Mended Wings
Love's Golden Wings
When Love Filled the Gap
To Love a Runaway
A Single Worry
Two Scars Against One
The Fiddler's Song
The Artist's Quest

Pioneer Romance:
The Wooden Heart
Heart-Shaped Pieces
Light in the Evening Time
To Strike a Match
Love's Velvet Chains
Destiny's Winding Road

Historical Romance:
So Swift the Storm
So Long the Night

Historical Novel:
Thread's End

Western:
The Other Side of Jordan
To Even the Score

Path of Promise:
The Broken Bow
Ordered Steps

Children's Short Stories:
Batteries for My Flashlight

Nonfiction:
Mother Eve's Garden Club
Heroes, Sheroes, and a Few Zeroes
I'm Coming Apart, Lord!
Alpha-Toons

Order from:
Pentecostal Publishing House
8855 Dunn Road
Hazelwood, MO 63042-2299

Mister B's Land

by LaJoyce Martin

Mister B's Land

by LaJoyce Martin

©1998 Word Aflame Press
Hazelwood, MO 63042-2299

Cover Design by Paul Povolni
Cover Art by Bill Myers

All Scripture quotations in this book are from the King James Version of the Bible unless otherwise identified.

All rights reserved. No portion of this publication may be reproduced, stored in an electronic system, or transmitted in any form or by any means, electronic, mechanical, photocopy, recording, or otherwise, without the prior permission of Word Aflame Press. Brief quotations may be used in literary reviews.

Printed in United States of America.

Printed by

Library of Congress Cataloging-in-Publication Data

Martin, LaJoyce, 1937–
    Mister B's Land / by LaJoyce Martin.
       p.   cm.
    ISBN 1-56722-222-6
    I. Title.
PS3563.A7286M57   1998
813'.54—dc21   98-34552
                                                                                       CIP

Contents

CHAPTER 1	Mister B's Land	7
CHAPTER 2	Gilla	17
CHAPTER 3	Diverse Thoughts	27
CHAPTER 4	The Awakening Soul	35
CHAPTER 5	An Effort at Distraction	43
CHAPTER 6	The Trip	51
CHAPTER 7	Furlough	59
CHAPTER 8	Music?	67
CHAPTER 9	Heartening Information	75
CHAPTER 10	Cassandra	83
CHAPTER 11	Death Notice	91
CHAPTER 12	Nightmare	99
CHAPTER 13	A Visit to the Lawyer	105
CHAPTER 14	Dawn	111
CHAPTER 15	Surprise Discovery	119
CHAPTER 16	A New Purpose	125
CHAPTER 17	Home Again	133
CHAPTER 18	Dismissed	141
CHAPTER 19	Tough Love	149
CHAPTER 20	Miss Joseph	155
CHAPTER 21	The Doctor's Report	161
CHAPTER 22	War!	167
CHAPTER 23	Two Calls	173
CHAPTER 24	The Bequest	179
CHAPTER 25	Lost Dreams	185
CHAPTER 26	The "For Sale" Sign	191
CHAPTER 27	The Letters	195
CHAPTER 28	The Return	203
CHAPTER 29	The Voice	209
CHAPTER 30	Reunion on Mister B's Land	215

ONE

Mister B's Land

All of G. Wilson Brumley's clan had taken their feather pillows and moved to the cemetery for a long nap . . . and there were several folks who wished the old man would join them there. Promptly.

In the first place, G. Wilson Brumley, known by the townspeople as Mister B, had outlived his expiration date by some two decades. "No one should hang around for ninety-three years!" the wishful ones vented.

Second, although his body had atrophied normally for his age, his mind had neither grown moldy nor clabbered by the turning of the calendar's pages. Mentally, he could still outbest the best. That didn't set well with the death wishers either.

Dozens of avaricious businessmen enviously eyed the old man's property, which squatted a mile and a half southeast of town. But like Naboth in the Bible, he refused to sell it, trade it, or otherwise sacrifice it to the gods of commerce. When one pesky investor pointed out that Mister B's rotting shack sat "right smack in the path of progress," G. Wilson just smiled.

"Progress can go 'round me, I reckon," he chirruped. "Ayup, it can just bypass 'round. I was here first."

A laughable antic had occurred the previous

MISTER B'S LAND

Halloween. Laughable, that is, to everyone except the disappointed land sharks. Some mischievous pranksters stole a real estate sign and posted it at the corner of Mister B's place. Under the words "For Sale," they chalked in "CHEAP."

The next day, the one-lane road in front of the old man's lean-to was filled with Hudsons and Nashes and Studebakers and new Packards. G. Wilson seemed to enjoy the joke immensely. "Why, I hain't had so much comp'ny in my whole short life," he chuckled. "Now that you fellers are here, why don't you stay and fish for a spell? I allow I can scare up poles aplenty for us all." No one ever got away from G. Wilson without an invitation to fish.

Some red faced, some angry, but all irritated, the dreamers returned to town. For a solid week, the telephone at the Albriten Real Estate office rang off the wall. The secretary wished she had a phonograph record that said, "No, the Brumley place is *not* for sale!" so she wouldn't have to bother with answering the calls.

"Red-tag the old place," insisted an eager member of the city council. "It isn't fit for a varmint to live in!"

Had the land been inside the city limits, it would have been a small matter for the housing authority to condemn the cabin and to move the antiquated man out. The dwelling boasted no paint, no plumbing, and no modern conveniences. But to stretch the city's skirts all the way out to Mister B's quarter section of prime river-front turf for the sole purpose of evicting him would have been far too obvious. Even disreputable men want to appear fair and respectable in the eyes of others.

Since Mister B had no surviving heirs, speculation was that it was but a matter of time before the industrial

MISTER B'S LAND

buzzards would swoop down on his little haven and pick it to pieces. After all, he couldn't live much longer.

The old-timer had never married; his sister and her only child had long slept underground. G. Wilson expected he would live out his life in peace, fishing when he chose, eating and sleeping at his leisure, honoring God and country. His needs were few, his expenses minimal, and his "rheumatiz" tolerable. During his lifetime, it seemed he had been long on friendship and short on friends, had given more than he had gotten back, but it had not embittered him. Grudges weren't worth toting.

Mister B did not know that, in fact, he had an Ahab in his life. This Ahab's name was Gilbert Carmichael. On occasion, Gil had visited him, making generous offers for the acreage, but the oldster was spared the details of the scheming, the plotting, the making of blueprints, and in short, the determination of Mr. Carmichael to get his hands on the envied site. It would mean time and it would mean waiting, but in the end it would mean money. Pyramids of money. Why, a hundred warehouses could be built along the waterway, generating a staggering income!

This smooth-tongued Ahab had even promised to put G. Wilson in a new home with water that ran from a faucet and a light that sprang from the ceiling, plus round-the-clock care, in exchange for his primitive one-room cottage. But what would an old woodsman do in a fancy house, squeezed among others just like it? He would suffocate, that's what! No, he wanted to feed his birds, talk to his squirrels, and pick his wild dogwood blossoms until he crossed over Jordan.

When Gil Carmichael made his calls, he never failed to inquire about the old man's health. Had he chest pains?

MISTER B'S LAND

Shortness of breath? Swollen ankles? Did he need transportation to the doctor? No, Mister B said, everything seemed to be working fine with the exception of the rheumatiz, but his own pappy lived to be a hundred in spite of the same bothersome blight.

A hundred? That was seven years off, and Gil Carmichael couldn't wait seven years. He was an impatient man; he needed money now. However, stoning or poisoning or drowning his enemy was out of the question. He couldn't chance spending an earthly forever in prison.

Now and then when Gil dropped by, he suggested that Mister B might need exercise. Would he like to walk about? To the river, perhaps? If the old gentleman suspected the younger's motives, he kept it to himself, but it is doubtful that Mr. Carmichael's subterfuge escaped the discernment of Mister B. Little did.

Along the banks of the river, Gil's mind always worked overtime: a loading dock here, a shipyard there. A wharf . . . a pier . . . The spade of his imagination dug foundations while his mental ruler measured and parceled and calculated. In this dream was a hundred grand the first year.

"This is a good spot for bluegill." Mister B had a way of interrupting delicious daydreams.

"Blue—? Oh, yes. Fish. With fins and scales. Listen, Mister B, if you will sell me this shoreline, I will have someone bring you to the river to fish every day for the rest of your life."

"Why, I reckon I can stay put right on my place and fish as often as I pleasure." The old man blinked innocent eyes. "Ayup, I'll stay. Nobody will be botherated to fetch me!"

MISTER B'S LAND

"But don't you see? I need this liquid highway for my business. It will increase my profit a hundredfold."

"Are you hungry, sir?" The gentle fellow's question came quite abruptly.

"Hungry?"

"Have you et food today?"

What had this to do with the real estate conversation? Mister B had decided to change the subject, or—oh, joyful thought!—he was indeed becoming senile. If he lost his wits, certainly he would need to be admitted into a hospital and his assets sold to pay for his confinement. . . .

"I say, did you have any vittles today?" repeated Mister B, a little louder.

"Yes, I had lunch in town before I came."

"And I notice that your shoes are in good repair."

Mr. Carmichael gazed at his shoes. "They're new. I bought them last week."

"Then with food and raiment be content," advised the old-timer. "Sufficient unto the day is the evil thereof."

"Ah, the Bible," nodded Gil. "That is a good book, and it quite proves my point. The wise Solomon admonishes us to get what we can from life while we are here since that is our portion. He collected lands. He had riches. He owned a shipping business. . . ."

"Was Mr. Solomon happy, sir?"

"With all his millions, he must have been. He was the wealthiest man on earth, I understand."

"Ayup. And one of the most miserable." Mister B shook his hoary head. "He groused that it was all a pester—his money, his livestock, his property, his ambitions. He wished, in fact, that he had never seen daylight. I wouldn't name that contentment, would you?"

"Solomon's problem was too many wives to support," countered Gil. "Can you imagine buying bath salts for seven hundred women? The man was wise, but he wasn't smart. He defeated his purpose. I dare say his wives spent his money as fast as he made it. I won't have that problem. I have no wife."

"Sir, if you will heed an old codger who has seen a heap of years, I can tell you that happiness is not tangled up in chattels. Another dollar won't bring you one whit more joy. A lust for the world's riches genders discontent. And if one had money past stacking, he still could be quite empty inside. This, sir," Mister B made a sweep over the virgin woods with his withered hand, "is life's crown: God's grass, a blue sky, too many stars for the seeing, and quietude."

"For you, that may be true," argued Gil Carmichael, his smile fixed and his patience draining out behind it, "but not for me. I can close my eyes and see—"

"I know. I know," the old man took up the sentence. "Smokestacks. Noisy motors. Tin buildings. Business, business, business! That's all you merchantmen ever think about. It is a sin, sir. Tell me, when is the last time you wormed a hook and held a cane pole in your hand?"

Mr. Carmichael gave a sawed-off laugh. "It has been several years. Since boyhood, I guess. I haven't time—"

"You haven't time to live. Sit down, sir," commanded the man in his nineties. "Today you will live again, and you will not forget it." From behind a nearby oak, Mister B extracted a pole and a rusty can. "Shall I bait, or will you?"

"Oh, really, Mr. Brumley, I must—"

"Here, I'll do it for you."

MISTER B'S LAND

"But—"

"Now, right there by that big jutting rock, there will be the fattest bluegill to ever grace an iron skillet. Watch the bobber, and when it bobs, jerk the line up." He put the pole in the professional's reluctant fist.

Mr. Carmichael certainly hadn't planned to humor the property owner to this extent. But who could tell what might tip the scales in his favor? If he won, it would be worth a few minutes of angling on the bank, for a few minutes is all he would stay. Wasted time was wasted money.

As Gil's hands held the pole, his thoughts continued to plot the industrial girders. A river on one side of his manufacturing complex and a feeder railroad on the other would spell certain success. Transport by land and by sea. Imports and exports. Factories and plants. Oh, he could taste the sweetness of prosperity!

He felt moronic sitting here holding a stick, but he had to have this land. He couldn't chance offending the old fellow and losing to someone else. Gil chuckled. If bait the old fellow he must, then so be it. He was the hook; the old-timer the worm. He'd sit on the bank and be ready to jerk when the time came. And he would have his "fish."

Any day now, his lucky break would come. The one who found the old man dead would have the advantage. He must check in more often.

Gil jumped when the end of his pole plunged toward the water. "Jerk, sir, jerk!" yelled Mister B, hobbling toward him. "She's a big un!"

Reflex made Gil react, and a flopping fish landed on the bank at his feet. "Oh, sir, she's a beauty," crooned the old man. "Ayup. A pound if she's an ounce. Now, the best way to cook her is to roll her in a little cornmeal and—"

The fish glimmered, wet and resplendent, in the dappled sunlight of the early afternoon, and as Mr. Carmichael looked down at it in surprise, the old-timer's words drowned in a lake of memories. Momentarily, Gil forgot his reasons for being here. He was a boy again, barefoot and carefree. He had caught his first fish, a silver perch, and he was running along the bank toward the house to show his mother what he'd snagged. She ran to meet him, laughing. She said she'd roll it in cornmeal and cook it for supper. . . .

No! He didn't want to reflect! Those were happy days, but they were filled with poverty, and his family's name was not on society's "who's who" list. Those days were gone. He would not be duped by the drowsy peace that threatened to swallow him, taking with it the grappling, the pushing and shoving to obtain the one thing he must have: wealth.

A meager existence was history. Gil Carmichael would have money. He'd have prime rib at the Wallace with the mayor. He'd have the best of wine and a 10X beaver Stetson.

"I haven't time to fool with a fish," Gil said, his voice brittle around the edges. "You keep it."

With trembling fingers, Mister B removed the hook from the fish's mouth and threaded Gil's catch onto a forked branch. "She'll make a mighty fine supper," he said. "If you'll stay, I'll cook her for you."

"Oh, no, no!" Gil objected, doing battle with annoyance and exasperation. "Really, I haven't the time." He threw another glance toward the river and was relieved that the mercenary vision had returned. Bustling workmen rolling barrels down ramps, barking orders. Bells and whistles and clangs. Loading and unloading. And most of all, money. Plenty of it.

"I'll tell you what, Mr. Brumley," Gil Carmichael bargained on the way back to his vehicle, "I'll buy your land with a written guarantee that you can live on it exactly as you are from now until you die, whether it is ten more years or a hundred."

"No." G. Wilson Brumley's face broke into the inexplicable and maddening smile that belonged only to him. "I'm not interested in selling my land. I told Pappy I would never sell it. I expect that God will take care of its bestowal when I've gone to dust. He's smarter than I am. He can give it to whomsoever He pleasures, and it will be spanky with me."

Gil gnashed his teeth. He was no closer to victory than he was when he came. No wonder nobody liked the old fellow.

He sprinted the last few yards to his car, trying to shut out the sound of the voice that trailed after him. "And I hope that it may be a fisherman who gets it. Apostle Peter was a fisherman, you know—"

TWO

GILLA

Dad, I'm spending the night with Peggy Gossimer. Love, Gilla.

Notes such as this appeared frequently on the refrigerator, anchored by an ornamental magnet. As long as Gil Carmichael recognized the name of the town's upper crust, he made no objection. His daughter was in good company.

Gilla Carmichael was prancing toward seventeen. She had exchanged her saddle oxfords for high heels, her dolls for jewelry. Long arms and legs had finally harmonized into a graceful body; her bright chestnut hair and delicate complexion served her well. The way she held her place in society inflated her father's pride.

Gilla had been motherless most of her life. When she was three, her mother left town with the maestro of a traveling band, and the woman hadn't been heard from since.

Cassandra Carmichael's disappearance created a typhoon of gossip in the city. Tongues provided ear fodder for the rumor mongers. She loathed motherhood from the start, it was told, relegating her baby to nursemaids and tutors while she danced the night away. "Famous brand clothes fit well on her body," claimed a talebearer, "but infamous names were sewn in the seams of her character." Her friends, if she had any, didn't bother to defend her.

Gil Carmichael didn't shed a tear for his truant wife. He was too busy to nurture a relationship anyway. Fortune making consumed his time. Her leaving liberated him from the confines of marriage, set him free for philandering.

At first Gilla missed her mother, cried for her, but the purgative of childhood forgetfulness soon washed away the memories. Gil destroyed Cassandra's pictures and mementos and never spoke of her thereafter. He hired a nanny, and life went on as usual.

Gil considered himself an excellent father. His daughter skated on the sidewalks around the great building that housed his downtown office. He often stayed at his desk until late at night, at which time Gilla would play jacks in the floor of the marbled halls.

It seemed to Gil that she had grown up overnight. How time had flown! "Do you need a new ball gown, Gilla, dear?" he would ask, or "Have you a ticket for the opera this weekend?" A good provider of material needs he was, and that is what mattered. He hadn't time to discuss trivial concerns with her, and he was glad that she didn't demand it. His world was among the ambitious who worked long hours to get ahead. Here he was comfortable. Here he knew his greatest satisfaction.

Gilla's name and her picture were included on the society page of the local newspaper at frequent intervals; her father saw to that. She was on the honor roll at her private school and elected president of every club she joined, at whatever cost to Gil's pocketbook. It went without saying that many of these clubs her father formed, chartered, and financed himself.

At her father's insistence, Gilla entered beauty contests for miles around. She was pretty, but so were others, which spawned suspicions that the judges were bought with a price. However, none dared voice their opinions.

Gil read the note on the refrigerator again. *Gossimer.* Ah, that was a good name. Bill Gossimer, Peggy's father, was on the city council. Gil hadn't a worry, for his daughter always kept her word. If she said she would be at Peggy's house, that's where she'd be.

But Gilla wasn't a puppet. When her destination wasn't qualified, she might be one place when her father thought her another. He hadn't the leisure for house-to-house (or hour-by-hour) monitoring, and Gilla hadn't a notion to be thus monitored. That's where the trouble began.

Young men had noticed Gilla since she was a budding fourteen, but she hadn't returned their attention. Lately, though, her father had begun to nudge her toward advantageous dates. "May I escort you to the ball tonight, Miss Carmichael?" became a standard invitation from the sons of the city fathers, many of these calls being prearranged. Gilla soon learned that she could pick and choose. Eenie-meenie-miney-moe: the most handsome, the richest, or the most popular. For a while she enjoyed the flattery, but then she became bored. The suitors were all the same. Artificial. Fawning.

Except for Judo. Judo was different.

His name was really Jude O. Franklin, and he said Franklin was German for "free man." Gilla liked his forthrightness, his manner of being completely honest. But Gil Carmichael didn't like him. Judo didn't cotton to the rules of society. He didn't try to make an impression on anyone.

And he wasn't wealthy.

Judo didn't like parties. He didn't dance, and he didn't drink. Money wasn't his master, nor did the opinion of aristocracy mean anything to him. He squandered his wages fighting for the weak, the unpopular, and the oppressed.

"What do you see in the loser?" hounded Gil, who loathed the boy's altruism. "You must cultivate friendships with the progressive and liberal-minded gentlemen who play an important part in our city."

The young man's unconventional behavior intrigued Gilla. She gloried in his spunk. He opened some window that had been closed and let in a breeze of fresh air. It was like an aroma of flowers to one who had ceased to believe in flowers.

Judo didn't present a card when calling. He had a habit of bracing himself against the mantel or a door frame because he disliked folding himself formally into a chair. Instead of bringing hothouse bouquets, he picked wild blooms for Gilla from the fields.

"What are these vile things?" her father once asked when he espied a clump of honeysuckle that his daughter had tenderly arranged in a bud vase.

"They're flowers, Dad," Gilla defended.

"Where did they come from?"

"Judo brought them to me."

"Bah!" he roared. "They are nasty weeds!" With that, he dumped them into the trash bin.

"Dad—!"

"If a young man cannot bring you proper nosegays from the florist, he shall not bring you any at all! Only cheapskates bring that which costs them nothing."

GILLA

"But I like them!"

"Well, I don't, and this is my house. My daughter will not be treated like a common milkmaid."

"They are pretty."

"Do not contend with me, Gilla. This has nothing to do with beauty. It is the principle of the matter that concerns me. You are the daughter of a civic leader, a prosperous man. If a gentleman cannot respect me enough to provide the very finest for my daughter—and at a considerable cost—he shall be forbidden to befriend you."

The reasoning made no sense to Gilla. A flower was a flower, from wherever it hailed. In fact, she thought it rather sweet that Judo should take the time and trouble to pick them just for her. Anyone could bring commercial blooms! Judo had made her feel special by his personal efforts. What had position, pomposity, or pride to do with human feelings? Couldn't a friend give a gift from the heart without society's frown?

As she matured, Gilla's confusion proliferated. She didn't blend with the crowd about her. Even when some of her friends were there, they were not present. They were in the moment ahead or in the moment behind. No one seemed to understand her. Except Judo. When she confided that she didn't want to fit herself to someone else's pattern, he told her he felt the same way. How did one find the essence of life? Nothing in the world, she sighed, seemed to be leading to anything of significance.

Gilla's soul had awakened and was asking questions. "What is church for?" she asked her father.

"It is God's house, and it is to learn about God, dear," he replied, looking over the financial section of the newspaper, dismissing the subject.

They were fine words, but when her father slept through the sermon and awoke to make business deals in the vestibule, she wondered at the establishment's fulfillment of purpose. God's house? Scant mention was made of Him in His own house.

Her education met with the same travesty. Grades stood second in importance to her popularity. If one or the other must suffer, let it not be her social standing. The whole of life seemed a path of revolting superficialities. Couldn't she do something different? Start somewhere else? Achieve something independently?

Judo was the only anchor in her storm, alive and true-hearted. He called on her often, but after the flower episode, she was careful to mix him among other "proper" gentlemen to stanch her father's objections. She was afraid that her father might expunge Judo from her life, and she needed him for balance.

Then Judo stopped attending church. When Gilla asked the reason, he said, "There is nothing there, Gilla. No spirit. Can't you see? God doesn't go, so why should I? I can feel more peace sitting on the park bench watching the ducks."

His answer might border on blasphemy, but Gilla agreed with his effrontery. He had put her thoughts into words. "Are all churches alike?" she asked.

"Oh, no! But you, Gilla dear, dare not break out of the traditional quagmire."

"Why, Judo? Why?"

"Your padded pew is conscripted for the rest of your life."

"Why can't I make my own choices?"

"You would be disowned."

"By whom?"

"By your father."

"He doesn't enjoy church either. He snores through every service."

"But there is a bottom line to all of it, Gilla. In this instance, it is money. M-O-N-E-Y. It is to your father's advantage to rent his pew. It brings him business. It is the church for the wealthy. Therefore, your father will not abide you going elsewhere. It would damage his image."

"Have you ever attended another church?"

"It is unfortunate that you asked, but I cannot lie. I went to another last Lord's Day."

"What was it like?"

"It was marvelous! The music was alive, the prayers fervent, and the sermon vibrant."

"Did you join?"

"No. It isn't a church that may be joined by the signing of a card or the shaking of a parson's hand. There are no programs and no paid seats. Anyone may attend who wishes and may worship freely."

Hunger roiled up in Gilla. "Where is this church?"

"Don't even think about it, Gilla. It is on the wrong side of town."

"I want to go."

"No! I will not take the blame for your heresy."

Gilla was accustomed to having her way. If she persisted long enough, she had learned, her father would humor her whims. Judo had aroused her curiosity about a different religion, and she wanted to investigate it for herself. Of course, Gil Carmichael would indulge her.

Or so she thought. However, when she mentioned it to the social royalist, he flew into a tirade such as she had not witnessed prior. "I forbid you to step foot inside another church, Gilla Carmichael!" he thundered. "In our church you will be wed. In our churchyard you will be buried. It is settled. Your name is on the roster with everybody who is anybody in this city. There will be no heretics in this family—" He stopped, narrowing his eyes to slits. "Who invited you elsewhere?"

"No one."

"No one indeed! All tares are planted by an evil spade, and I think I know who that rascal might be. Have you discussed religion with that Judo fellow?"

"Only once."

"As I thought."

"But he—"

"He is a snake in the grass."

"I just asked him why he hadn't been coming to our church lately."

"And he told you he had joined another?"

"No. He couldn't. That is, the church he attended doesn't take joiners."

"Ah, yes," mocked Gil. "The 'whosoever will' kind. They'll take the scum of the earth, the run-down-at-the-heels sinners, the poverty bitten—"

"Judo says those are the ones for whom Christ died."

"Wrong! Those are the ambitionless, shiftless, irresponsible bums! They cohabit with mice, lice, and vice. Our church wouldn't have them! We turn those kind down every week. Why, they would take out of the offertory instead of putting anything in!"

"Judo said—"

"Enough! I don't care what Judo said. He is tainting your pure mind with heathenism, and I will not tolerate it!

GILLA

You are never to speak to that young man again. Never! Do you hear?" He was shouting to the top of his lungs.

"I hear you, Dad. You're screaming at me."

"And you will obey."

Gilla dropped into a pool of silence. She didn't plan to make a promise she could not keep, for she had fallen in love with Judo. Her allegiance was now with him.

Gil jabbed a finger toward her. "If I catch you disobeying—"

"Then what?" Her look challenged him.

"Just don't try me, Gilla. You shall not disgrace me. If you do, you'll wish you hadn't." He spun on his heels and walked off, the sound of his boots cracking hard against the polished hardwood floor.

Whether or not Gilla would have contested the command of her father will never be known. She hadn't the chance. War clouds hung on the horizon, and Judo left her a note that he had joined the army to serve his flag. It was something he must do, or he would be no man at all, he said.

THREE

Diverse Thoughts

"Happy birthday, Gilla!"

Gil had been harder on his daughter than usual. When she had challenged him on the church issue, he had let his ire get the better of him. All children had inquisitive minds, and he shouldn't have overreacted. Now he felt guilty and a bit remorseful. After all, his daughter was a social pawn that he couldn't afford to lose.

He feared he had come dangerously close to alienating her from himself; she had been quiet and withdrawn since he yelled at her. But he was glad that Gilla had seen it his way. She hadn't questioned religion again, and she took her pew regularly each Sunday.

To make amends for his sternness, doubtless unfounded, he bought her a 1936 Ford Cabriolet, complete with running boards and a rumble seat. It was a used model, for Gil was not as well set as he would have people believe. He'd be able to buy her a new, custom-built roadster when she graduated from college, at which time he would have Mister B's land and the wheels of fortune would be rolling. But this year he had already borrowed to pay his income tax, and he would have to work all next year to repay that loan.

Gil parked the Ford in the driveway and watched with

satisfaction as Gilla's eyes glowed with delight when he told her it was her birthday gift. His chest swelled when she caressed the fenders and patted the hood. Ah, he had his girl back again! Gone was the sadness in her eyes that nothing seemed to erase. Almost (he shuddered) had he backed down and told her she could speak to that dreadful boyfriend again. Almost . . .

A letter had appeared in the mail from the boy, and Gil opened it. The young man was off on some military lark, playing up the hero image. He told Gilla he would not forget her and that she was to wait for him. After reading the letter, Gil tore it to shreds, and Gilla never saw it.

"You will teach me to drive?" Gilla was grinning.

"What? Oh, yes, certainly."

"Today?"

"I have one hour, dear. I have scheduled an appointment with a shipping magnate. The meeting stands to bring me much revenue." He paused and smiled. "But you are intelligent. You can learn all about the clutch, the gears, and the brake in an hour. The wheel comes naturally. It is no harder than steering a bicycle."

With one foot propped on the running board, Gil pointed as he spoke. "Okay, there are three pedals down there. The left one puts the car in neutral, the middle one is the brake, and the one on the right is the foot feed. Press the neutral pedal all the way down to put it in gear. Then gradually let up as you press the gas pedal. The stick in the middle operates the gears. Down and toward you is low. Up and toward you is reverse. Up and away from you is second, and down and away is high."

"How will I remember all that?"

"Draw yourself a diagram of a backwards N in your

DIVERSE THOUGHTS

mind. Always start in low, go to second, then to high."

He took her out of town for practice, telling himself that he should be headed for his office and not to some dirty country road. But she was an apt learner, never making the same mistake twice. He would be through with the teaching in an hour.

They came to the edge of G. Wilson Brumley's 160 acres. "It is beautiful out here!" she cried. "I didn't know what I was missing by being cooped up in town."

"That," Gil jerked his thumb toward Mister B's land, "is a piece of property that I want very badly."

"Then why don't you buy it?"

"It isn't for sale."

"I've never known of anything my father couldn't get if he tried hard enough."

"I've tried hard enough, all right. I've begged, bargained, and pleaded. But it happens to be owned by an old goat who won't budge. A family promise. He is ninety-three, and no amount of money will sway him."

"Well," Gilla suddenly sided with the owner, "I don't blame him for not selling his land. If I was ninety-three and had lived under those lovely trees for a lifetime, I wouldn't sell either. Even to Gil Carmichael."

Gil snickered, a laugh that thinly covered his frustration. "My only hopes are that he won't live long and that I can get it when he is gone."

"His children might have a say in that."

"He has no children, no heirs. He is a bachelor."

Gilla drove back to town and deposited her father at his meeting place. "You'll do fine with the driving," he said absently, his preoccupied mind ready to put aside the intrusion of a daughter's birthday.

MISTER B'S LAND

Feeling a need for more driving practice, Gilla returned to the country road. With her own motorcar, she could go where she pleased. Oh, for someone with whom to share her elation! If only Judo were here . . .

Mister B, leaning on his hoe handle, threw up a friendly hand. Few cars made dust on his road.

Gilla tried the brakes, sliding to a stop. As G. Wilson inched toward the fence, Gilla jumped from the car. "My! You have a nice place here," she said, smiling. "I love springtime."

"Ayup, girlie, 'tis a special place. It belonged to my pappy. He was here afore Texas turned itself into a state. He said when he came upon this cove, he knew how the children of Israel felt when they saw their promised land. He staked claim on this stretch and lived it out. He always allowed the sniffing of fresh-turned earth could make you forget what botherated you. It could find what you had lost, fill you up where you was emptied. Ayup, he claimed coming here put a full set of hair back on his head.

"I cut my teeth on the saplin's here, girlie, same as the beavers. I had a tree house in that big oak," he flapped his hand toward a large tree, "and a swing in that one. And I've been contented here. I promised Pappy I wouldn't see it mauled and turned into a modern scurry as long as there was breath in my body.

"Pappy lived to be a hundred, and I sore miss him yet."

"I'm Gilla Carmichael, and I am out learning to drive," Gilla told him. "I got a car for my birthday. My father pointed out your place to me."

"Ayup, it has been home to me for ninety-three years. And I'd admire to tell you that it has sustained me well.

DIVERSE THOUGHTS

Anything will grow on this place. I've fruit and nuts and berries right on the land to go along with the garden I upraise every springtime. With my little pension, I manage goodly. Since Pappy died, it has been just God and me; we get along with each other. We have some long talks, the two of us."

"You talk to God?"

"Ayup, girlie. Every day."

"What—what do you talk about?"

"I talk to Him like you'd talk to your best friend. I tell Him everything that botherates me and everything that pleasures me. Don't you talk to God?"

"N-no. I didn't know one could."

"Oh, you poor, poor girlie! God allowed anyone could come to Him. He has a ready ear." The old man gave a toothless smile. "But now you know you can."

"I think it would be easier to talk to God out here in the country, away from the busyness of the city. Don't you?"

"Ayup. One of my favorite places to visit my Master is down by the river. Would you pleasure to walk down to the water?"

"Oh, I'd love it very much!"

"So how old are you today, girlie?"

"I am seventeen."

"That's a goodly age. That's how old Joseph was when God commenced that great work in his life."

"Joseph?"

"Joseph in the Bible. He is my favorite character. Besides Jesus, of course. Joseph was betrayed, demeaned, and bedeviled by his own brothers, but he held no vexation. He floated right back to the top no matter

MISTER B'S LAND

how he was cast down. Read about him when you can, girlie. He is in the Bible's beginning book. Genesis."

"I will," Gilla said. "I will read about him tonight."

They had reached the river. Lazy water lapped at the shore like skeins of blue silk while birds gave soft concerts all around them. "It's most nigh holy here," the old man said. "In the arms of God's creation, earthly frets fade. That's why Pappy and I lived so long. When a bluegill is nibbling, it is hard to be botherated about the stock market."

"A bluegill?"

"That's God's most glorious table fare. Have you ever been fishing, girlie?"

"No, sir."

"And for shame. Well, here on your birthday, you will experience a forgetless pleasure. Sit on that big rock there." He tilted his head toward a boulder.

Mister B produced a pole with a hook waiting for bait. "I'll ready it up for you," he said, attending to the details before handing Gilla the fishing gear.

"Now," he instructed, "drop the line just yonder from that branch that sags out over the water. When you feel an urge on the pole, yank it up quickly."

Fascinated, Gilla obeyed. In less than a minute, she pulled a thrashing fish from the river. She squealed with girlish delight. "I caught one! Oh, look, sir! I caught one!"

The old-timer appraised it with practiced eye. "It is most nigh as big as the one your paw caught."

"My dad fished?"

"Indeed he did, girlie. Caught a full pounder. I fried that baby and et him for supper. Couldn't get Mr. Carmichael to stay and share the feasting. He allowed he

DIVERSE THOUGHTS

was too busy. His taster don't know what it missed."

"May I try to catch another?"

"Help yourself. I'll do the baitin' as long as you pleasure to fish."

Gilla caught several more, but her mind was distracted. *Her dad fishing?* There must be a side of him she didn't know. So this is why he wanted the land . . . ? He longed for the peace, the solitude, this feeling of timelessness. . . . He needed a respite from the hassle of the hectic business world. And this would be just the place! A tender emotion for her father filled a space in Gilla that had been hardening. The mental picture of him sitting here holding a pole warmed her heart.

"What will happen to this lovely spot when you are gone, sir?" Gilla's genuine concern disqualified rudeness.

"I don't know, girlie. I am turning it over to the Maker of it to decide. I hope that it may always be a haven for the weary of soul."

"I hope so, too," she agreed.

That night, Gilla told her father about her day. "Oh," she babbled, "the place you wish to buy is a most wondrous place! I know why you want it so desperately now. I understand. The old gentleman took me down to the river and—"

"You saw it then? You saw the awesome possibilities?"

"And I felt it, Dad. As I stood on the bank—"

"Ah, Gilla. With that tract of land, I would be a millionaire overnight."

"Yes, Dad. Money can't buy the tranquillity one finds there."

Gil didn't hear her. He was lost in another world, a world of raw commercialism. He picked up his coffee cup and set it down again. "I can close my eyes, dear daughter, and see the potential: warehouses and docks and pulleys and chains. Booms and cranes. Shipping and loading and freighters. Factory roofs stretching as far as one can see. I tell you, I can make a fortune with that property!"

Gilla looked at her father strangely. Her stomach tipped. She opened her mouth to speak.

But Gil talked on, animated now. "If the old man would just drop dead. He claims his father lived to be a hundred. If he matches that, it will be seven years before I get my hands on that shoreline. Seven years! And here I sit like a wet weekend! Competitors could beat me to the punch by then. I need the property now."

"But, Dad—!"

"It's true, Gilla. I know it sounds cruel, but a spent generation has no right to stand in the way of an unspent one. I offered to situate the old man in a nice townhouse with perpetual care in exchange for the place. But, no! He is determined to grow his muscadine grapes until he turns to petrified wood! I even promised to let him fish from one of my wharves—"

"I see." Gilla's words were flat as was the hope in her bosom that she might find a trace of humanity in the man she called Father. The whole color and shape of her day changed. The shovel of disappointment dug trenches in her soul while her young heart ached with bruising sadness for one who thought only of making another dollar.

Gilla felt the moisture of unshed tears prick her lashes. She hoped her father didn't get Mister B's land.

FOUR

The Awakening Soul

"They say when one commences to relive his life, he is scarin' the end of it," G. Wilson said to no one at all, "and I have been rewindin' the spool of thread all day long."

He had been born in McLennan County on the Brazos River in 1848. "Me and the gold rush hit at the same time," he'd oft chuckle, "but, of course, you can guess which was the most important."

He had one sister already fifteen years down life's road when he arrived. She married young, a mere sixteen, and bore one son, Paul. Paul, unorthodox from the start, was a strange boy who turned into an even stranger man. Some claimed he wasn't "all there," but G. Wilson contended that there was "too much there." His genius made him a misfit in society, causing him to wander without purpose or direction.

Paul talked to himself and was obsessed with the New Testament's Paul of Tarsus, his namesake. He wrote pages and pages of commentary on the apostle, eventually publishing the exegesis in a book. Nobody bought the books; therefore, Paul gave them away to many an unwilling recipient.

The man didn't believe in owning anything. He proclaimed himself a missionary of sorts and meandered afoot from place to place, finally exiting the world by way of malaria on one of his "missionary journeys."

G. Wilson had one of those extinct books and had worn it threadbare trying to get to the core of Paul's ramblings. What was his nephew trying to say? There must be a method to the madness somewhere. Perhaps, he decided after numerous readings, he could furnish the book with a purpose for existence since Paul had miserably failed to do so. But how?

Looking back, G. Wilson accounted that adolescence took up an exorbitant portion of his life. In his mind it stretched over a vast period, holding a foretaste of life's inevitable tragedies and the struggle to understand them. At eighteen years of age, he had fallen in love.

Rose Willis was his one and only sweetheart. They had grown up a farm apart, both shy and self-conscious. Young and innocent, they had known a love that could not be duplicated. There would never be another in this world or in worlds to come.

In 1868, he had written in his journal: *There is fullness of life where my Rose blooms. Her presence makes a cold day warm. My heart follows her about as one might follow a moving patch of sunshine. She is my touchstone. Every joy, every sensation is multifold when I am near her.* He was twenty then, she nineteen.

For years, G. Wilson had kept a letter from his Rose and had read it every night. Now the letter rested between the pages of Paul's book, too tattered and faded to be legible. Or was it his dimmed eyesight that rendered it unreadable? The best he could do was piece together every detail he could remember, no matter how small, in

THE AWAKENING SOUL

hopes that the choppy recall might keep alive the indescribable feeling he'd had long ago when in her company.

The end came for Rose in 1869 just three weeks before their wedding day. A horse spooked. A shay crashed into a tree. And a young man's beribboned hopes were lost with the snuffing out of his espoused.

A part of G. Wilson died with Rose. He was heartbroken, empty, inconsolable. Why did it happen? He asked the same question over and over in hopeless repetition while great gusts of realization buffeted him. She was gone. *Gone.* Nothing remained for him but remorse—picturing, imagining . . .

But grief cannot long stymie youth. Time eased the pain, and G. Wilson invested his energy into the land. He had claimed the plot beside Rose in the cemetery as his final resting place, vowing to remain true to her memory. In a way, she had been right with him all these years. Sometimes he caught himself talking to her.

All in all, his hadn't been a bad life. He'd had his share of health and good fortune, savoring the river, the soil, and God.

At this point in his reverie, he felt a nap coming on. It was time to fold the years, smooth them, and put them away. But first, the prayer. "God," he implored, "please, don't let this beautiful land become a cesspool of steel and iron. Let it not be ravished by road graders and dirt movers and heartless machinery. Then what would become of the baby rabbits and the chipmunks and the woodpeckers? Rosie couldn't have borne the land being spoiled, nor can I."

A timid knock on the door startled him. He seldom had visitors, and as slowly as his arthritic joints moved, his caller would be gone before he could get out of his chair. "Come in," he called. "The door is unfastened." G. Wilson, trusting soul, had no lock on his door. He hadn't a thought in his heart that anyone would harm him.

Gilla stuck her head in. "I'm sorry to disturb you—"

"Oh, no, no, girlie. You aren't disturbing a thing," croaked Mister B through a sleep-lined mouth. "As long as you're sitting behind my walls, those fishies won't get a case of nerves. Come on in."

Gilla looked about. The bleak surroundings thrust her into another world, another era, a place she had never been. A lump choked her throat. This poor old man had nothing. A rugless floor. An old iron stove. An apple crate that held a few chipped cups. A sagging mattress and a chamber pot. Yet he had something she did not possess, something elusive for which she would trade all her earthly comforts.

Was it possible that only once in a lifetime you caught a glimpse of truth? If so, would you find your hand empty when you tried to grasp it? No, because now you knew it was there, and once stretched, your mind could never return to its original proportions.

She, Gilla Carmichael, had the best of earth's trappings. A late-model car. A canopy bed with silk adornments. Fine clothes and perfumes and jewelry. But she was bankrupt, for she felt no fulfillment inside. The old man had found peace that wealth could not purchase.

"I didn't come to fish today, sir. I came to tell you that I read your Joseph story." Her eyes traveled to the Bible that lay open on a three-legged milking stool beside Mister B. A magnifying glass made a portion of the page's print stand out in large letters.

THE AWAKENING SOUL

"Ah, it is a fetching story, yes?"

"It is, sir. And I feel there is something in it for me. Yet I don't understand how it could apply to my own life. I have no brothers, I have no fear of being sold into slavery, and my father would never be beholden to me. There is no parallel, you see."

"Ah, girlie, the ways of God are past finding out. If, indeed, He has a lesson for you there, He will make it plain. Don't fret yourself. In truth, Joseph's story points us to Christ, our Savior."

"In what way, sir?"

"Jesus was betrayed by Judas and sold for thirty pieces of silver like Joseph was sold. And just as Joseph became the savior of his family, Jesus came from death's prison to be our Savior. Don't you see?"

The words were simple, but Gilla knew so little about the Bible that such simplicity is all she could have grasped.

"Yes, I do see!" she said, her eyes lighting with the tiny pinpoint of revelation. Then, with yearning she uttered, "I wish I could be like Joseph. He was so forgiving."

"Ayup. And so is our Lord," Mister B said. "It is through His forgiveness that we can be pure and holy."

Pure and holy? Gilla felt neither. "What do you mean by pure and holy, sir?"

"Free from sin, clothed in God's own righteousness. You see, no unclean thing can enter heaven," he explained. "Without God's cleansing, we are all unholy, as smelly as a skunk. Would I welcome a skunk in my house? Neither would God. We must separate ourselves, soul and body, from this world. The apostle Paul allows we are to present our bodies a living sacrifice, holy and acceptable unto God."

MISTER B'S LAND

Gilla had never heard that verse of Scripture, and her conscience was pricked. Had she presented her body to God? Oh, she had presented it—in various stages of immodesty—to the earthly judges, a recurrence that had been troubling her for some time. But of what use were beauty contests if she was not beautiful to God?

The question came of its own volition; she must know. "How do you feel about beauty contests, sir?"

"I think they are shameful, girlie. Young ladies were not purposed by God to be exploited, their bodies gaped upon, and their fair faces worshiped for their outside comeliness. God intended women for a higher goal, to be His handmaidens. One's real prettiness is inside. The packaging counts for pennies."

It was a bare statement, presented with honest directness, and Gilla appreciated it. Decisions long in the deep freeze of her soul began to thaw. She went home determined to settle an account with herself.

Gil Carmichael caught his daughter poring over the Bible that evening. "What are you doing, Gilla?" he barked. His abrupt query hung in the air by some fine edge of feeling not yet visible.

"Reading."

"Looking for something in particular?"

"Yes, I was trying to find the verse about presenting your body to God."

"I don't know what you are talking about, but you must not interpret the Bible for yourself, Gilla," he warned sternly. "Self-interpretation leads to all sorts of errors. If you have a theological question, we will take it to the rector. He teaches from a modern viewpoint. Much of the old text is not for us today, anyway. The Bible is an

THE AWAKENING SOUL

archaic book not to be taken literally; it must be taken figuratively." He stopped, and his voice cut the air. "Have you been speaking with Judo again?"

"No, sir. He joined the army. He is gone."

"Well, close the Bible now. We have something exciting to talk about."

The Book closed slowly. "What?"

"I've entered you in a special beauty pageant. Your winning will put you in the big leagues. Miss Texas. Miss America."

"Dad, I—"

"There are three categories. Formal, semiformal, and swimsuit. The swimsuit category counts for the most points, and that is where you will shine. I'll see that you have the finest bathing suit that can be purchased."

There was no smile on Gilla's face, no enthusiastic response. She dropped her eyes, aware of the intangible coercion her father had placed upon her in the last few months.

Gil misread her actions. "You needn't be afraid, Gilla. You will ace it!"

"I'm not afraid," she said, lifting tortured eyes. "I just don't want to be in a dumb old contest. I don't ever want to be in a beauty contest again."

Gil's jaw muscles bunched. "What is the matter with you, Gilla? You are being pettish." He did not recognize the page that had turned in his daughter's life.

"It is a personal conviction, Dad."

Gil was angry. He clenched his teeth against his seething irritation. The idea that he might be losing his hold on Gilla was intolerable to a nature as possessive and power bitten as his. "Personal convictions, bah! As

MISTER B'S LAND

long as you are in my house, Gilla, you will amount to something. At seventeen, you are under my jurisdiction, and I will not allow you to become a Bible-studying prig. Is that understood?"

She nodded. A very slight nod.

FIVE

An Effort at Distraction

Gilla didn't win the beauty contest. She wasn't even a runner-up.

It was one of those rare occasions when her father could not attend the affair, and to say that he was upset when he learned of the results would be a woeful understatement. He was livid. He accosted a member of the judging team, a personal friend of his, the next day at lunch. "Why didn't my daughter win, Jack?" he shot.

"She didn't try, Gil," his friend replied.

"What do you mean she didn't try? I bought her the finest swimsuit—"

"Gil, in order to win a contest of this magnitude, a girl must have, er, vivacity."

"And you are saying Gilla doesn't?"

"I'm saying that Gilla hadn't one ounce of emotion about the whole thing. She had no spark, no life. She didn't even smile. You have been to enough contests to know that a gal has to have some degree of 'come hither' to get the judges' votes. I voted for her because I am your friend, but she had no other votes. It was almost as though Gilla didn't want to win."

"Had something upset her?"

"I don't know." Jack hesitated before he went on. "Gil,

it is obvious that something is eating at the girl. It likely had nothing to do with the contest."

"She has nothing to be disturbed about."

"No?"

"Did she seem ill?"

"I don't think she is physically ill."

"Just what are you inferring, Jack?"

"I think it is a heart thing, Gil. You've provided for her, financially at least, and you've done well. But she is missing something in her life. It might be her mother."

"Now, Jack—" Gil's face reddened.

"You asked me; I'm telling you. It's probably her age. A child can go along for years, and then suddenly, there it is: a void. A sense of missing a part of herself for which she must search. This happens with adopted children and orphans. It is nothing new."

"Gilla has never mentioned missing Cassandra."

"Of course not. She wouldn't want to seem ungrateful for the care you've provided. She loves you and appreciates what you have done for her."

"She doesn't even remember her mother, Jack."

"It makes no difference. Fantasy dredges up all sorts of things to plague a child's mind. Look, Gil, raising teenagers is no picnic. They are complex mysteries to themselves and to everyone else. I just said it *might* be her mother. It could be something else, something that has nothing to do with the past. Our children are frightened by all this talk of war."

"Gilla isn't a fearful child."

"It might be a hunger for emotional fulfillment, a craving of the mind. Music or art or poetry. Have you ever read Florence Nightingale's story? She had an inner call-

AN EFFORT

ing to be a nurse but was afraid to tell her family. Maybe your daughter wants to be a singer or an author or an actress. She is unfulfilled, Gil. You can see it in her eyes. You are a brilliant man, but you are aloof and remote, wrapped up in your career. Be careful, Gil."

"Of what?"

"Shutting out your daughter."

Gil bristled. "I haven't shut out my daughter. And if anyone says I have, it's not true."

"I'm not saying you do it consciously or deliberately. In life, it is the little things that count. We say 'I love you' in a thousand ways. And you haven't time for small things. Have you ever sat and talked with your daughter about her mother? Is it fair to her to destroy the memory of her mother? Whatever Cassandra did to you, she was Gilla's mother."

Gil's banked anger broke over the dam of reserve. "Better no mother at all than one like Gilla was cursed with!"

"You're angry with me."

"I am. You are falsely accusing me."

"I'm not accusing you."

"You're telling me I haven't been a good father to Gilla. Who appointed you my judge?"

"You asked me, Gil. Please don't ever ask my opinion again if you are afraid of truth."

Gil lowered his head. He breathed a heavy sigh and looked at the floor. "Okay. You may be right, Jack. I have sensed a bit of defiance in Gilla lately."

"That's one of the first symptoms."

"Symptoms of what?"

"Depression."

"What should I do?"

"A change of scenery sometimes helps. You might get her away from here for a while to give her a chance to find herself."

A cloud rolled across Gil's face. "I haven't time to flounce about the country with a sentimental daughter. I have business to take care of, money to make. The way this war is cranking up, I see opportunities unlimited for us businessmen, and I plan to enjoy my share of the fallout." He hesitated, realizing he'd just proved Jack's point. Then weakly he murmured, "Tell me how to do it, Jack. I can't just abandon my job."

"Hire someone to take her. You need a break from her, and she needs a break from you. Obviously, you are dancing on each other's nerves."

"Have you a suggestion as to where I should send her?"

"Oh, there are plenty of wonderful places! New York City. Padre Island. A ski resort. A dude ranch. Send her wherever she wants to go. It won't dent your pocketbook."

"I wish I could believe that it would work."

"It will." Jack slapped Gil on the back. "And when she returns, she will win every beauty contest in the state of Texas. I guarantee it."

His mind churning with grand plans, Gil took off fifteen minutes early and went home to talk with his daughter about her vacation. Other fathers were sending their prodigies on luxury cruises, to lands abroad, or on scenic tours. Why not he? And why hadn't he thought of this himself? Gilla was feeling inferior, underprivileged. That's it! That was the problem and easily enough solved.

AN EFFORT

He made up his mind to say nothing about the beauty contest Gilla had lost. That might further depress her. For some time now, the contests had proven a touchy subject. Better to avoid any mention of it. There would be plenty of time for contests when she gained the feeling of equality among her globe-trotting peers.

As he entered the sitting room, Gil found Gilla curled up on the sofa with the family Bible. Again! He was highly displeased, but he hid his chagrin well. This obsession with that outdated Book only substantiated Jack's reasoning that Gilla needed a change of pace, fresh surroundings. If a dull book like the Bible interested her, she was indeed bored. *It is my fault,* he thought. *I should buy her some contemporary materials.*

"You are home early," Gilla noted. "Are you ill?"

"I'm fit as a fiddle," he gasconaded, "and in high spirits. I just won a contract from Washington, D.C., and I'm wanting to celebrate! Unfortunately, I haven't the time. It's a deadline job.

"So I have chosen to let you celebrate in my stead, my dear daughter. I have arranged a trip for you. You may go anywhere you wish and may stay all summer if you'd like. You need a break before fall when, of course, you will enroll at the university to begin classes for your degree."

"Will I make the trip by myself?"

"Oh, no! I will hire an older woman to be your companion. But you shall have your own private room and personal freedom. You will be at leisure to pursue whatever interests you. You are old enough to make decisions on your own now."

"Will I be required to go to parties?"

"No."

MISTER B'S LAND

"To concerts?"

"No."

"To church?"

"No."

A tiny smile blossomed on her face. "Then I will go." Had the answer to any of her questions been yes, Gil deduced, his daughter would have balked. It was all a part of the complexity of maturing that Jack had pointed out. But get her away he must, for her sedition was growing teeth and fangs.

"Where would you like to go?"

"I think I'd just like to travel around by train."

"Across country here and there to sightsee?"

"Yes, sir."

"That should be interesting. But I'll need to know where you are intermittently."

"And what I'm doing?"

"No, I don't have to know what you are doing. That is your choice." Gil was saying all the proper phrases, and he knew it. He was proud of himself. Wait until he told Jack! (Once an objective had been accomplished, Gil liked to brag about it.)

"Thanks, Dad. I do need a break, some time to think."

"Right! And you will have full access to my bank account. Spend as much as you need to have a good time, but don't be wasteful."

"I won't."

"And write to me."

"I will."

The conversation pleased Gil Carmichael well. Jack was right; his Gilla would come back with new verve. By her eighteenth birthday, she would be ready to take the

AN EFFORT

city by storm. And if she wished to know about her mother then, he would tell her.

"You may go to your room to begin packing," he told her. "And if you need anything, let me know."

Gil returned to his office, bouncing through the door, and worked until night pressed its dark face to the windows. He stopped frequently to give himself accolades for his exemplary fatherhood. Gilla would reward him by making him proud of her, winning for him many contests.

Part of his duties as a conscientious father was to distract Gilla from her recent religious bent. Get her mind off the Bible; it was a parasite. He had seen girls wreck their popularity with piety. He would not let Gilla go down that road. Never!

Gilla went through her wardrobe, selecting only the most modest of her clothing. The plunging necklines, the bare backs, the strapless gowns were cast aside. She filled three trunks and then went for her Bible. It would go in the top of her last case.

But her Bible was nowhere to be found. In its place was a book entitled *In Tune with the Times: A Guide for Modern Women*.

She left it lying.

SIX

THE TRIP

"I will be a guardian but not a dictator," Claudette told Gil Carmichael. "I will protect your daughter to the best of my abilities, but I refuse to police."

"That is as she wishes, madam," Gil said and hired her.

From the start, Gilla got along with Claudette, a middle-aged woman who tried to hide time under a thatch of hair dyed inky black. One never had to wonder where Claudette stood on an issue; she made her position clear.

Her last name was Cyszyec. "Just sneeze twice, and you'll have the right pronunciation," she suggested. As a former governess for the county's juvenile hall, she knew her business.

"May I just introduce you as Claudette Sneeze?" picked Gilla.

"Please," she folded her hands into a beg. "We shall get on royally. I can smell a wild spirit for a mile; you haven't one. You will do as you wish, and so will I. I've never been paid so much to do so little."

"I wouldn't purposely give you fits, madam," Gilla responded.

"There you go already!" Claudette scolded. "I'm not 'madam,' I'm Claudette."

"Yes, Claudette."

"And, by the way, where are we headed on this train?" Gilla hunched her shoulders. "Any suggestions?"

"How about Colorado? I've always wanted to go there."

"That's as good a place as any."

"At least it will be cool there."

At the train depot, the Gideons were distributing Bibles. Gilla reached for one eagerly, but Claudette shook her head when offered one. *God has ordained this trip to reveal hidden truth to me,* Gilla concluded. *This Bible is proof.*

It was out of character with her workaholic father to make room for a vacation or even to think of one, leaving Gilla further convinced that a Higher Power was at the helm. Had Gil Carmichael insisted that she do things his way, as he usually did when he sponsored a venture, she would have refused to make the trip. Had he demanded that she accept invitations to parties or go to dances or attend a church of his choice, the voyage would have been canceled. But he had surprised her by attaching no stipulations, no strings.

The train chuffed in with a rush of wind that swirled Gilla's skirt about her legs, rolling to a grinding stop. Not sure where to board this display of headlong power, she glanced from engine to caboose. A porter, clinging to the iron rail of the last car, dropped to the platform and came toward her, wreathed in servile smiles. "Let me have your baggage, and this way, if you please, ladies," he bowed.

He showed them to a passenger car, and shortly the locomotive headed north, clanking and swaying into the forest that circled the town, following a path of crossties and tracks.

THE TRIP

Beyond a long trestle that spanned the Brazos River, the engine gathered strength, and they were on their way. The tight wires of tension in Gilla's chest slackened to a more manageable degree of pressure.

Why had her father not mentioned the beauty contest? She was glad he hadn't because she had planned to tell him it was the last, that she didn't feel comfortable parading her scantily clothed body in front of a bevy of ogling judges. Her principles would be compromised no longer. For him or for anybody.

Her father had pushed her into a corner for the last time. He could make black seem like gray with a little talking; with a lot, he could make it seem white. But she had come to realize that even though he could make things seem gray or white for a while, they were still black in the end. What God wanted she did not know, but she was beginning to learn what He didn't want.

The trip passed quickly and without rail delays. In Colorado, Claudette arranged for a mountain chalet, behind which burbled a stream of icy water. "The best drinking water in the state," the real estate agent crowed. "One hundred percent pure." They moved in, and for the next few days while Claudette cooked and embroidered, Gilla sat in a rattan chair beside the stream and read the entire New Testament, making notations on a tablet.

She found the verse of Scripture about being holy of body, to which Mr. Brumley had referred, and studied it intently. According to the verse that followed, some transformation must take place, but she didn't know how that would be accomplished.

Gilla's long silences and deep thought prompted Claudette to ask if she felt well. "I feel okay," responded

Gilla. "I'm just trying to get some things straight in my mind. Are you knowledgeable about the Bible?"

"I know too much about it," quipped Claudette. "My grandpa was a fire-and-brimstone preacher. I got my fill of religion long ago."

"Can you explain a verse to me?"

"Oh, no! That was one thing your father specified. I am not to discuss the Bible with you. That was the purpose of your trip, I was told, to get your mind off such matters. Your father wants you to drift through the next few weeks without the burden of serious contemplation. To have fun."

"I see." Gilla did see. She saw that her father's plans for this trip and God's plans clashed.

"I have some contemporary books if you would like to read them. Some tell-all romances."

"No, Dad promised I could do as I pleased. And I am pleased to do more reading in God's Word."

The second week, Gilla started on the Old Testament. When she got to Joseph's story, the same strange stirrings filled her, a sensation that there was a specific message here that involved herself and her future. If she could but find it!

At the end of that week, she wrote her father a note describing the terrain. It was a wilderness of mighty peaks, she said, much of which hadn't seen the foot of man. The aspens and the evergreens were magnificent. She would be here a little longer, she penned, then they would move to another location. He would be posted as to their whereabouts.

When she finished the letter, she scanned over it. She had told him nothing about herself. Not that he would

THE TRIP

notice or mind. Armored in his self-interest and thirsty for gain, he would pay little heed to her letter anyway. He'd read it in a panic lest the few minutes spent in the perusal might interrupt his long communication with his own desires. Recently birthed was an awareness that he loved her not for her own sake but for his sake. He could not love what he could not control.

A dispatch ricocheted from Gil Carmichael by airmail, special delivery. The missive was rather long and scattershot. He was glad that she was having such a wonderful time. (Had she said anything about having a wonderful time?) He praised her for her choice of scenery. She must see the Garden of the Gods and the Royal Gorge, he said. Colorado Springs was a resort for the more popular movie stars, and he hoped that she might meet some of them. Give them his regards, especially if she saw the king, Clark Gable.

He noted that she had written few checks, and he scolded her. Entertainment was expensive, but she certainly was not to cut herself short to spare his pocketbook. There would soon be more money pouring in than either of them could spend, he assured.

The letter rambled on. Negotiations were under way for a windfall. The government would build a munitions plant if he would supply the land and would manage the manufacturing detail. Then the army would buy the ammunition from him at a grand price! It was a no-lose deal with Fort Hood just an hour away.

Of course, he would have to have land situated for shipping. "Oh," he wrote, "if the old-timer would only die today!" He had been to see the old gentleman again, but he couldn't detect any death rattle about his person.

MISTER B'S LAND

Mister B had asked about Gilla, calling her Lady Joseph, with some strange ideas about her "floating to the top." Perhaps the old fellow's mind was weakening. When the mind went, the body usually followed.

Peggy Gossimer had her picture on the society page of the newspaper. She was engaged to be married to the mayor's son and would want Gilla to be in her wedding, of course. It was the talk of the town.

"The new bank president, Mr. Fitzwaren, arrived this week," Gil scribbled. "I attended a dinner in his honor. He is such a prestigious individual that no amount of special information detracts from or adds to his air of importance."

Gil went on to say that Mr. Fitzwaren had an eligible son. He ended by remarking that he personally bore the olive branch by contributing a bottle of his expensive port wine, which was enjoyed by all. A postscript noted that a host of invitations awaited Gilla on her return home.

Home. Had she ever had a real home? What would it have been like to have a mother? The old, sad aching stirred in her; the loneliness and longing came alive like gray embers flaring in a gust of wind. She remembered the soft kid glove she'd found behind the dresser. Supposing it belonged to her mother, she had hidden it, taking it out now and then to hold to her cheek. Vainly, she tried to recall sitting in her mother's warm lap with arms about her. What she did remember was whispering to her doll, hugging to herself the meager comfort of the inanimate fabric. Thinking about it sent a knot to her stomach that hurt; a tear crooked its way down her face.

Home. The word unveiled no cozy pictures for her. It was a hollow chimera, and just now she felt a million ages

THE TRIP

removed from the eight-bedroom Maple Street dwelling that housed her and her father. The letter from her dad gave her no pang of homesickness. It worked rather the opposite.

The days fled by, and Gilla felt that she was gaining nothing. She had finished reading the Bible, but most of it she did not comprehend. Surely, she was missing some spiritual endowment; the undisclosed truth that she sought was still buried. How would she ever unravel the mystery? Would her soul be forever hungry? If only Judo hadn't left! And why hadn't she heard from him?

Restless, she could not settle on any diversion. Weary with the bleakness of her hours, she roamed the nearby woods. But nature no longer solaced her; the mountains failed to quench her thirsting spirit. Where should she go now?

"You're losing weight, Gilla," Claudette complained. "This will never do. Your father will hold me accountable. Are you bored here? Would you like to go somewhere else?"

"Yes, I am through with Colorado," agreed Gilla. "Let's move on." She packed her clothing, wishing God would tell her which direction to go and would let her know when she had reached the next phase of her journey. Mister B said she could talk to God. Now was as good a time as any to start.

SEVEN

FURLOUGH

Jude O. Franklin had drawn an overseas assignment. It looked as though the animosity between nations was leading to a world war that could involve the United States. Germany's dictator, Adolf Hitler, had sent armies into Poland, igniting the fires of battle around the globe.

Jude had been granted a week-long furlough before shipping out. He wanted to see his father and Gilla, for from the looks of the war, he might never return.

He went to his own house first, holding the door open with his foot while he removed the key from the lock and dropped it into his pocket. Then he stepped inside, letting the door close behind him.

"Hi!" he called. "Anybody home?"

There was no answer. He hadn't really expected any. From where he stood in the entrance hall, he could see into the living room with the light of day's end striping in through half-closed blinds. The room looked exactly as it had all his life. He supposed his father was off on a business trip as usual.

The young man felt sorry for his father, a man who couldn't fathom where he went wrong in the rearing of his only son. The senior Franklin owned a prosperous pub and traveled far and wide to procure the best liquors for his store. He planned for his lucrative business to be a father-and-son partnership, but Jude wanted nothing to do with wine, the tasting, or the selling thereof.

Eventually, Jude's father had given up on him, encouraging his decision to join the army. Mr. Franklin was of the opinion that if Jude couldn't fall in step with society's demands, it would be best for him to make a quiet exit.

Girls had never interested Jude. They were all shallow, mindless actresses clamoring for attention, divorced from virtue and wed to popularity. Except Gilla Carmichael. She was different. A field flower dressed in its natural beauty meant more to her than an expensive waxed rose from the gift shop. She disliked the artificiality of parties as much as he. He had found in her a kindred spirit.

But she had not answered his letter. She had ignored it. That thought cut deeply. However, there was the slightest chance that the letter had been lost in the mail; she may not have received it. He would see her during his brief intermission from the service to appease his mind. Why not today?

At Gilla's residence, Mr. Carmichael was rushing out the door, briefcase in hand. Jude met him on the steps. "Hello, Mr. Carmichael," he said, extending a hand.

Gil nodded, ignored the outstretched hand, and tried to rush past Jude. But Jude blocked his way. "I have come to see Gilla," he said.

"Gilla is out of town," clipped Gil.

"When are you expecting her return?" Jude pressed.

"It will likely be several weeks before she comes home," Gil scowled. "Gilla needed a break before she begins her college studies."

"Did she get my letter?"

FURLOUGH

"She did," lied Gil, "but since she has no interest in cultivating your friendship, she dismissed it."

"Is—is there someone else?" Jude had to know before he faced death.

"Yes."

"Thank you, sir."

Now he knew. Gilla had played with his heart, his emotions. She led him to believe that she cared for him, but . . . out of sight, out of mind. To toss her into the heap with all the other flighty girls was the hardest thing he had ever done. Now, if die for his country he must, he could not carry to his grave the memory of a loyal girl with a waterfall of chestnut hair and honest blue eyes. *She had found someone else!*

With heavy heart and slow steps, Jude went home and slept for the rest of the day. When his father had not returned by the next evening, he went to the pub—a place he loathed—to inquire about his whereabouts. The bartender said Mr. Franklin should be back in a week, the day after Jude's leave ended. Jude would miss seeing him, and it was perhaps his last chance.

While Jude was in the abominable tavern, his notice took in a glassy-eyed man, staggering drunkenly, wandering from one table to the next. Gil Carmichael! As Jude watched, Gil stumbled and struck his head on the corner of the bar, breaking his shot glass and cutting his head.

"Oh, sir, are you all right?" Jude was at his side in a trice.

Gil struggled to focus his vision on Jude. "Go away," he said thickly. "You led my daughter astray. You told her to read the Bible." He gave an inebriated guffaw. "But she won't read it anymore because I threw it away. When she comes home, she won't remember it or you."

"Please let me take you to your home, sir. You are in no condition to drive."

"Mind your own business, whippersnapper. I can drive Gilla's car. I'm fine. And I'll be finer yet when the old man dies."

When the old man dies? Mr. Carmichael wasn't making sense.

Jude waited and then hailed a taxi to follow Mr. Carmichael home, praying that the besotted man would make it there without an accident. In his own driveway, Gil passed out at the wheel of the Ford. Jude found the man's house key, took him inside, and put him to bed.

The first two days Jude spent in his hometown were days of hurt and disappointment. He hadn't expected a grand welcome, but he had hoped for a placid respite before he faced his uncertain future. Aimlessly he strolled, walking along the river, his thoughts churning, his restiveness driving him further and further from the din of the city.

The voice brought him up short. "Hullo, sonny. What's the haste? Sit a spell and fish with me. If you hurry up through life, you'll come to its end before you pleasure."

Jude looked up to see an old man clad in overalls and worn-out boots sitting on a mound of shale, a cane pole beside him. His hair was the color of old cobwebs. "I allow if you're too busy to fish, you're too busy. Fishing has a fancy of soothin' one's fever, and you look like yours could stand soothin'."

Jude dropped down beside him. "Indeed it could, sir. I came here to find peace, and it looks like you have found it."

FURLOUGH

"Ayup, sonny. What more could one ask of God than His good air to breathe, the song of birds, and the music of a river? Folks nowadays ask too much of life and pay the awful price of worry for the asking. God never allowed that His children should have a fret. Most of this modern generation don't know the spelling of riches, I dast. Godliness with contentment is great gain." While G. Wilson exhorted, he strung a pole for Jude. "What is your name, young man?"

"My name is Franklin, sir, and I am home on furlough."

"Furlough, eh? We haven't joined the war, have we?"

"We're headed there on a greased slide, sir. Hitler is making havoc for all mankind. We've tried to stay out of it, but it is my feeling that we will be forced into the fracas."

"Here, sonny," the old-timer handed the pole to Jude. "Fish a spell. Your heart begs a rest."

"Thank you, sir."

Jude said nothing for a while. Sitting on the ground littered with spots of sifted sun, he let the tranquility of the water take its effect.

"You seem like a right nice chap," G. Wilson said conversationally. "Do you know the Lord?"

"Yes, sir. He's my friend. The only friend I have right now."

"You can count me as your other friend if you'd pleasure," Mr. Brumley said. "Thatwise, both of us would have two. I'm quite alone since the girlie departed. I miss her sorely."

"Your granddaughter?"

"No, just a visitor. She came often to fish and to talk

about the Bible. She particularly cottoned to the story of Joseph. I got to naming her 'Miss Joseph.' She hungered for righteousness, but afore our friendly got full grown, she went away. Gilla was her real name, and a right fetching lassie she was. She was kind of heart and gentle of spirit. That kind is rare nowadays."

"Gilla?"

"Mr. Carmichael's daughter. The man has a lust for earth's wealth. He covets my land. But the girl is not thataway."

"Where did the girl go?" The question, nearly suffocated, was wrung from Jude. Before it escaped his mouth, he wished he had quenched it.

The old man chuckled. "I had a letter from her this very week. She is in Coloraydo studying her Bible morning, noon, and evening. And 'tween times, too. Now won't that create a fearful kerfuffle for her unbelieving paw?

"It was a bit amusing. I hadn't got a letter from nobody for twenty years. The rural mail carrier fetched it to my door personal. He said he figured it must be mightily important!"

"She went away to Colorado to be married?" Again, Jude wanted to bite his tongue for the excessive preoccupation shown.

"Oh, no! She had a beau who left for the army. She hadn't heard a peep out of him since he departed, but she didn't skip a day thinking on him. She favored me to say a prayer every day that he would be safe, and I've minded my bargain to do that."

"She didn't mention his name, did she?"

"She called him Judo. That's a right unusual name, don't you think? But believing Miss Joseph, he was the truest and most noble man God ever set afoot on earth. If right she be, God will bullet-proof him and hie him back to her shipshape, for I know she loves him."

EIGHT

Music?

A full orchestra of prosperity! A man heard the music of opulence only a few times in his life, and Gil Carmichael strained to catch the prelude now.

It seemed that he could hear the city growing and stretching. It was a curious illusion, the thwack of hammers, their beats synchronized, the air heavy with the smell of sawdust and fresh paint. Every falling hammer, every turning wheel brought him closer to the culmination of his dream, an industrial empire of his own.

Now at the end of the day, he sat at his desk, looking out the fourth-story window of his office. He had a grand overview of the city, spreading like a lava flow to the fields, the farms . . . and reaching its tentacles toward G. Wilson Brumley's property.

He compared the city to a family in the process of remodeling its house, throwing away the old furniture and getting newer and more modern upholstery to replace it, refurbishing everything. Everybody wanted to remake their world—businesses, houses, churches—on a grander scale. Old Mister B didn't understand it, couldn't accept it. All his generation understood was a slingshot and a fishing pole; they scowled at men who came with railroads around their necks and banks on their backs, heeding the

MISTER B'S LAND

call of big money. Mister B's ilk would choose a tree rotting in the woods before they would hand it over to supply a roof over a man. They couldn't realize that an oak growing was just an oak. Cut it up, and it's a house. Brumley was an echo of yesterday, of the century past. This was a new day. This was 1941.

Main Street met First to form the business section of the city. It was crowded with after-work shoppers. Halcyon days were here in this golden age. Among the tightly packed cars nosed in to the curb at the meters, scarcely one was more than five years old. Store windows displayed expensive merchandise. Traces of the Great Depression were gone. Forever gone.

Through a fringe of trees, Gil could see the river, glinting a metallic blue in the fading light. He closed his eyes to hear the strains of the orchestra, to envision a forest of smokestacks along the curving shoreline of the Brazos River. Cut down the trees! Shove chimneys to the clouds! Let the smoke write new lyrics for old songs, new music for old ballads! Mills first. Then furnaces. Then docks and ships. A stretch of railroad. Each step a triumph and, at last, sweet success.

Well, if death didn't take the old man soon, the city would run over poor Mister B. Gil would go to any extent—even to selling his house if need be—to get his hands on that slice of land.

"Are you asleep, Gil?" Gil jerked his head around. Jack laughed. "I thought for a minute that you were paralyzed."

"Just making plans, Jack." He pulled down the roll-top of his desk, locked it, and retrieved his hat from the ledge on top. The heat of the day had exhausted him. "Let's go for a drink to cool off. I owe you one."

MUSIC?

"Gil, you are drinking too much in your daughter's absence." The uncontrollable appetite for alcohol was transforming Gil's once strong body into the vase-shaped caricature of a fat man. He would soon have three chins. Even his most spacious suit failed to minimize the bursting effect on his belt line.

"I'll taper off when Gilla comes home."

"How is her trip going?"

"Marvelous! She wrote that she had never had so much fun in all her life. Parties. Meeting celebrities. More dates than she can fill. I'm glad I came up with that vacation idea."

"Where did she go?"

"To Colorado to a famous ski resort."

"Superb! She'll have all those religious traces kicked out when she returns."

"She's going to Florida next. To the beaches for a nice tan."

Jack whistled. "When she gets back, she'll knock the contest judges flat."

"She's having a heyday while I sit here and work, work, work."

"Knowing you, you wouldn't have it any other way." Jack's eyes fidgeted to Gil's file cabinets. "And just what sort of work are you doing now, Gil?"

A snort and a sneer met in Gil's nostrils. "I assess and collect taxes for the city. On commission. Most folks don't question the amount I affix. Some do. I've had to back off on a few, claiming an honest mistake in the figuring. You pretty well know who you can stick and who you can't."

"So I can expect my property taxes to go up?" gibed Jack.

MISTER B'S LAND

"No worries. Friends are exempt."

"What do you do about those who won't pay up?"

"I make them think they will lose their property, but, of course, if they are homesteaders, they cannot be evicted. Texas has a homestead law. Believe me, if eviction were possible, I would see G. Wilson Brumley put off the land he's been hogging for a century."

"Has he kept up his taxes?"

"Yes, sir! I keep his assessment to a minimum so there will be no delinquency when I take over. I'm nobody's fool!"

"Are you still holding out for that land, Gil?"

"Look, Jack. You get one chance in your life to step in when the elevator is going up. I can make a bundle just selling the lumber off that place. With this war cranking up, I'm going to manufacture supplies for Uncle Sam, and I can send them down the river by the ton." Gil laid his hat aside. "Let me tell you something. I was once a poor man, a nobody. I sat like ragged Lazarus at the gate of the rich, looking in. One day I decided I was tired of the dogs' lickings; I would be the rich man for a while instead of being the beggar.

"Nothing can exceed the longing of a poor man, beaten by circumstances, to rise above his poverty. With every beat of my heart, I can hear a throbbing in my ears that says, 'Go for it! To riches! High position! Fame!' And I'm getting there."

"If you don't tone down on the booze, Gil, you won't get anywhere."

"I have complete control of myself. I know what I am doing. I know where I am going. Drinking helps me pass the time until my big break comes. Then it will no longer be necessary.

MUSIC?

"What my daughter would not understand—nobody understands—is that I could not have gotten to first base in life with Cassandra as a noose. She was an albatross about my neck." Gil was saying things he had never voiced, but now that he had started, he couldn't stop himself. "She didn't want to be rich! Our goals were poles apart. She would have been content to live in a board and batting house for the rest of her life. I think she genuinely hated money.

"Furs and jewels meant nothing to her. She would never wear them, claiming them pretentious. Why, I couldn't even get her to use rice powder on her face! She loathed parties! Cassandra was shy of making new friends; changes alarmed her.

"I refused to be led or driven into becoming the man she wished me to be. A low Joe. Pious. Religious. An advocate of peons. If I couldn't have a woman who would rise with me, I preferred none at all. And I told her so."

"So in a sense, you drove her away?"

"I never would have divorced her. I am too much of a gentleman to put a woman out on the street."

"Then she asked for the divorce herself?"

"We are not divorced."

"You're telling me that you have been married for fourteen years to a woman who left you for another man?" Jack looked surprised and interested all in one trick of his heavy black brows.

"If I file papers, she can get half of my property and maybe my daughter, too. One can't trust the quirks of the courts. They're mawkish when it comes to mothers."

"And you haven't heard from Cassandra from that day until this?"

"I haven't."

"How do you know that she is still alive? If she were alive, don't you think she would have contacted you?"

"Cassandra has sent Gilla a birthday card every year since she left."

"And what is Gilla's reaction?"

"Gilla doesn't know about the cards. I intercept the mail at the post office the week of her birthday to make sure she doesn't get them."

"Is that fair, Gil?"

"Fair and square! When Gilla is an adult, I will tell her about the cards. But I have wisely chosen not to strap her childhood with a burden that is not hers to bear. It isn't her fault that Cassandra and I were not compatible, that we walked two different roads in life. Children don't want to understand, not completely. It is too destructive. They need some things left for imagination. I am handling my family affairs correctly, Jack. My way has been successful. My daughter, well-adjusted, well-mannered, and beautiful, will enter Baylor University this fall."

The dialogue deserved no reply and got none. Below, cars moved in dark flocks like migrating birds. "It is growing late, Gil. Let's go downstairs and settle for a cup of coffee."

When Gil Carmichael walked into his front door an hour later, he carried a brown paper parcel, wrapped tightly enough to define the shape of a bottle. He spread the mail on the table. A notice from the bank that his account was overdrawn. A letter from the utility company threatening to discontinue service if he didn't pay up at once. A dun from the finance corporation giving him an immediate deadline to fend off the repossession of Gilla's car.

MUSIC?

The veins in his neck stood out like purple ropes choking him with anger. Why couldn't his creditors wait a few more weeks? Didn't they know that before long he could buy the whole town and get back some change? The shoe would be on the other foot shortly, and he would be hounding them. Then they would know how it felt to be pushed.

In the meantime, he would have to impose higher taxes to cover his expenses.

He pulled the bottle from the sack. He had to get control of himself.

With the first swallow, the purple rope began to slide down into his collar.

NINE

Heartening Information

G. Wilson Brumley had invited his young guest to supper. It was the first time he had shared a meal with another human since his father died in 1911. He fried the fish that Jude caught, and they spent a companionable evening together. Well after dark, they still sat visiting.

Jude found serendipitous healing at the humble hearth, yet he had ulterior motives for prolonging his stay. He hoped to hear more about the girl he loved, be it fact or be it opinion.

"Your place is surely a sanctuary for a bruised soul," he mentioned to G. Wilson.

"Ayup," agreed Mr. Brumley. "Miss Joseph liked it here." Jude sat forward in his chair, but Mr. Brumley went on as if he had never spoken of Gilla. "In winter you can hear the frost talking, and in summer the wind gets tangled in the old shingles and blunders about trying to discover its way out. I grow my garden here. There's no fruit as goodly as a ripe bramble, fresh picked and et while the warm of the sun is still in it. I've always been light of money but heavy of God's blessings.

"Mr. Carmichael allowed he wanted to put me up in one of those fancy new flats where everything is tight squeezed and choked off with no elbow room and where

MISTER B'S LAND

you can't sniff the smell of grass or hear any birds' songs. But I nixed that.

"I'd admire to say that my little corner of the world is dedicated to God. What will happen when I am gone, I dasn't venture a guess. That will be God's problem. If I had my druthers, I would pleasure to see God keep it green and peaceful for fishermen instead of turning it over to a big machine that treads downs and pulls up whatsomever it touches."

"Can't you specify in a will or something—?"

"That would be snatching it out of God's hands, sonny. He knows what's His desire for this land. Mr. Carmichael wants to commercialize it. His mind churns on naught but dollars. I dare say he's counting the days until my funeral.

"Nor do I fear death, sonny. I fetched a title on a mansion many years gone, and I've paid my payments faithful. I expect I will enjoy God's house even better than my own here."

I'll be fine when the old man dies. . . . Jude's mind winged back to Gil's sodden words. This, then, was the man of whom he spoke.

"It would pleasure some folks to see this pretty river front corrupted with factories and machines and noise," Mr. Brumley sighed.

"And that would be a shame," Jude acceded.

"Ayup. Then no one could hear the birds' choir or the testimonies of the katydids."

"I hope your birds are permitted to sing forever, sir."

The old man got up to light a candle. "Franklin, how is it that you sit here and delight to talk to an old man with one foot in the grave? You have better things you

HEARTENING INFORMATION

could be doing, I venture."

"I need solace before I go to the battlefield, sir, and this is the best place I have found."

"You think it'll come to blows over yonder?"

"Yes. The United States can't stand by forever and see the smaller nations of the world crushed beneath the heels of power-hungry leaders. I feel it's my God-given duty to stand for what is right, and I have volunteered my services. The moment of truth is coming."

"Wonder will it be as bad as the last one?"

"I'm afraid so, sir. Maybe even worse."

"So they let you off to say your good-byes, eh?"

"Yes, sir. I finished basic training and am on a seven-day leave."

"Why are you not companying with your kith?"

"My father is away on a business trip. I won't get to see him before I'm shipped overseas."

"And your mother?"

"She is at rest with the Master; she died the year I started to school."

There was a moment's silence. "Ah, Franklin, may God journey with you. It is noble to stand for right or even to die for right. If I wing to the other side while you are gone, I'll look to you someday. Who knows? Maybe we'll meet up there real soon."

It had to be far past the old man's bedtime, but Jude longed to hear Gilla's name once more. A sudden rush of tenderness for her possessed him, along with a spasm of regret that he would likely not return from the war to see her lovely face.

"Tell me about Miss Joseph," he blurted.

The old man made a funny noise that Jude took for a

laugh. "She is a dandy, that un," he said. "I will never forget the day she came bumping down my dirt road in her fancy little horseless. Ayup, she slid the contraption ten feet trying to get it to whoa!

"I was out hoeing, and she favored me with a friendly hello. Now, it rubs against my religion to neglect a fishing invite to anybody that hails my way, so I asked if she would care to go for a fish. It was the first time I had asked a lady, and lo and behold, she took me up on my invite!

"And she snagged a beaut' right off; she did. I allowed she was natural born to be a fisherwoman!

"Catching that fish pleasured her so that she jumped up and down hollerin', 'I got one!' It warmed my old heart to see her girlish joy. You'd'a thought she'd just won a million dollars.

"I offered to cook it up for her, but she allowed if she didn't fetch her horseless back to town, her father would fear she had crashed it.

"But she came back, she did. Let's see, mayhap it was the next day. I can't recollect everything in order anymore. Some days my mind blurs, and my remembering feels like it is stuck with tape all over my brain. Then I can't convince anything to join up in a proper line.

"We talked about the Bible, the girlie and myself. I told her that my favorite man in the Bible besides Jesus was Joseph because no matter where you tossed him, he floated to the top again. She asked where the story was, and I said it was in Genesis.

"Onct she up and asked me what I thought about beauty contests. These old bones ain't nothing but honesty, so I confessed what I thought, that they were of the devil. And I spoke her Paul's Scripture about our bodies

HEARTENING INFORMATION

belonging to God for His glory and not for the glory of some public display. I allowed that weren't just put in the Bible to use up ink.

"Afterwards, every time she came, she begged to talk about Joseph. She said she had a down-deep whisper that the story was meant for her although she couldn't find out why. She hadn't been sold or wronged, nor had her father ever been beholden to her for the saving.

"Then she came one last time to say a farewell just before she tripped off on the train. She fetched me a sack of peanut butter cookies she had cooked up herself. It was a trip that her father desired her to go on—" the old-timer stopped abruptly. "Hmm," he mused. "Never once did the girlie mention her maw. Now that wonders me."

He continued, "She allowed she would want the same fishing pole when she got back from her trip because it knew where to tempt the big ones. That's the pole you fished with today."

Jude laughed. "Seems that it still works."

"She said she'd be harking back at summer's end."

"Would you mind giving me her address?"

"It won't do a tidbit of good to write her, Franklin. She will not gift you with a bidding chance. She has her heart padlocked on that Judo fellow, and nothing will loosen it. She'll have a match of her own whittling, that one will."

"But I know Judo pretty well, and I want her address for him."

"Well, why didn't you speak up afore? You know her Judo?"

"Yes, sir."

"Well, in that case," Mr. Brumley opened the yellow-paged Bible to Genesis and took out the envelope that

MISTER B'S LAND

was lodged between the pages. "Here 'tis. She will be mighty glad to hear from that young man, I warrant. And if he wins her, he will be a mighty lucky fellow. She has a heart of gold."

A draft played a trick with the candle, and the shadows danced. The old-timer's head doddered. The light of the flame played on his white hair, giving him a waxen pallor of death. He had said he was ninety-three. His days were numbered, or could he count by hours now? Earth couldn't hold him much longer.

Jude arose to go. "Come back for another fish tomorrow," insisted Mr. Brumley.

"I will do that, sir," responded Jude. "I would like nothing better."

The river looked like bean soup in the little chip of moonlight as Jude idled his way back along its shore. He could sleep tonight. And dream of Gilla.

In town once more, he let himself into his childhood home. Though his mother had been gone for sixteen years, the rooms still bore traces of her occupancy. His dad was one of those men who never bothered with changes. He had no interest in decor and was too busy with his bar to attend to superficial possessions anywhere else.

Hungry, Jude salvaged some leftovers from the icebox. He fried an egg, made toast from stale bread, and had some soup. Then he rustled up a pen and a tablet to write to Gilla. The paper and the scratchy noise of the pen made a wall between his thoughts and their expression. His words stumbled, and he hadn't a talent for penmanship.

Unsatisfied, yet feeling he had done his best, he

HEARTENING INFORMATION

walked to the post box and mailed the letter. The night had worn through to three o'clock when he crawled into bed, emotionally spent.

Jude overslept the next morning, a rare event for him. When he went back to the river, the old man was not fishing. With an intuitive premonition, Jude made his way to the cabin and found Mister B there. Dead. He had died during the night.

With a great sense of personal loss, Jude notified the sheriff and the undertaker. Then he posted a quick note to Gilla. She would want to know.

However, by the time his messages reached Colorado, Gilla was gone, leaving no forwarding address.

TEN

CASSANDRA

Needles of rain pecked at the window. Cassandra Carmichael pulled herself from the dregs of sleep, rousing to the haunting sediment of regret that met her every morning, refusing to withdraw. She'd had a bad night. And now the rain. Rain always made the pain worse, the memories more acute.

She looked at the clock. It was 8:30 a.m. Thomas had left for work two hours ago; the stockyards opened at seven.

She reached across to the bedside table and opened the drawer, rummaging about for a tissue. Instead, her hand fell on the birthday card. It was crazy to buy a birthday card a year ahead of time, but she had seen it in Woolworth's five and dime store and had known it would be perfect for her daughter's eighteenth birthday. But why mail cards year after year? In all these years, she had received no response from Gilla.

A weak tear brimmed over and tracked an irregular course down her face. She wiped at it with the back of her hand. Then down went her head into her pillow, and she sobbed. Not for today alone but also for the barren yesterdays and the bleak tomorrows.

The mental doors she had tried to bolt shut swung

open as though jarred by a rude gust of wind. With time's telescope, she slipped back to Gilla's third birthday—the last she'd had with her baby—and she saw the child as clearly as if she was in the room with her. Big blue eyes. Golden curls. Little dimples like doodle bugs' indentations in the sand.

Was that the day she had made the awful decision to leave Gil, the prelude to fourteen years of horror, confusion, and misery, years of questioning over and over in hopeless repetition?

She was looking back on another life. A huge gulf separated her from the years with Gilbert Carmichael and her precious little girl. Had there been a night that she hadn't awakened to listen for a child's cry, waiting for the cold blue of morning to dispel the nightmare? Did one ever get over the sickening, heartbreaking chasm? Would she go wild with the inner ragings to which she had become a victim? She was so tired, so lonely.

Had her whole life been one tragic mistake? It seemed to Cassandra that for as long as she could remember she had been confronted by situations with no solution. She had been orphaned at ten years of age, along with her two older brothers. No one wanted three youngsters, so they were separated and put up for adoption. She remembered the terror of it all and how she hid under the porch, hunched over, arms clutched around her body to try to diminish her fears. A woman she did not know found her and scolded her harshly.

Cassandra's adoptive mother, chronically tired and out of humor, treated her like a dose of medicine that must be taken. She favored her own children, dressing the "extra kid" in shabby hand-me-downs. The entire family

CASSANDRA

took shocking advantage of Cassandra, making her do sevenfold the work of the other members.

In adolescence, Cassandra began shutting herself into her private world of fantasy, beautiful dreams of love and admiration so different from the reality. These dreams sometimes brought real tears to her eyes. She believed that someday they would come true.

Then when she was sixteen, she met Gilbert Carmichael. They were picking cotton in the same patch on a crisp Saturday morning. Would she ever forget that day? She started off dragging her sack behind her, the cotton burs snagging her fingers. Before the first hour was out, her back hurt miserably.

She and Gil weighed in at the same time, and he had twice the pounds as she. "A pretty girl like you ought not be in the field," he said with a rakish grin, and her heart was smitten. He was physically strong and suntanned, and his fast-talking abilities served him well.

He proposed marriage the third time he called on her. Eager to be free from the burden of another mouth to feed, her adoptive mother signed for her to be married. Cassandra was barely seventeen; Gil was twenty-two.

Even now, her mind tried to evict the disappointment of her wedding day. They had gone before the judge to say their vows. When the nuptials were spoken, she turned to Gil with radiance and joy only to see, with marrow-chilling shock, that he was bored. Bored at their wedding! His mind, she learned later, was plotting and planning ways to fit her into his scheme of climbing the rungs of success's ladder.

She loved the man so much and understood him so little! It was a terrible exposure when she learned that he was dishonest, that he would lie, cheat, or deceive to get ahead. Before she married him and for a little while afterward, she thought him clever. Any man who could make circumstances appear different from what they really were must be a smart man. Later, she realized it wasn't cleverness. It was a character flaw of seeing things not as they really were but as he would like them to be.

When she gently chided him, he brushed away her concern with an amused and patient look. This was the method in which the business world operated, he told her. It was a dog-eat-dog affair. "Anyway," he claimed, "I'm trying to make it easier for you."

Put in those terms, it made her feel ungrateful for saying anything negative. "I just wish you didn't have to take advantage of other people. Why don't you go to school to be a doctor?"

"It takes too long. Eight, ten years." Gil wanted quick money. "I want to be rich now while I'm young enough to enjoy it," he said, taking her by the arms and lifting her high in the air.

He went from one sales job to another. Hang a promise in front of his nose, and he was off like a schoolboy chasing rainbows with a butterfly net. All of the "opportunities" were wonderful, sure-fire pursuits that couldn't miss. But they did.

When Gil got his way, he came home with flowers and candy and promises. Big promises. But when he didn't, he could get nasty and mean.

Gil kept saying he wanted to be somebody, to get somewhere in the world. However, all Cassandra wanted was a peaceful home, love, and a family. Their ambitions collided. Gil made plans to attend dances, balls, and din-

CASSANDRA

ners. Cassandra felt out of place at these soirees. She especially disliked the flirting that seemed to be acceptable at such functions.

Gil wanted her to dress garishly, wear bangles, and apply heavy makeup. She liked simplicity. If she did not meet his demands and she was not the belle of the ball, he would rant long into the night. She would fall asleep with his voice in her ears. If shouting didn't wake her, he would shake her back to consciousness to listen to him. "Cassandra, listen to me! Do you want to ruin my whole life, every chance I have for a brilliant future?"

The more she retreated into herself, the greater his harangue. Soon she didn't have to listen. She had all his lines memorized. Still he wouldn't let her rest, so she had to sleep in the daytime while he was gone.

Yet all of it she took patiently—the battling, the pounding, the sleeplessness—because she loved him and because eventually things would change. She would have her happy family.

Two years after their marriage, Gilla came to join them. Cassandra knew a few days of untarnished happiness. She spent her time in joyous motherhood, hoping Gil would now excuse her from the parties. But no. When she was well enough to be out and about, he insisted that she hire a baby-sitter and accompany him again.

She couldn't leave her baby with strangers, she said. Gil's peers would understand. Her stubborn determination matched his. Motherhood was her priority. He would get over his petty notion when he saw that she wouldn't truckle.

But he didn't. All at once the arguing stopped. Everything stopped. He became silent and morose, breathing sighs and staring at the walls. She thought he was sick.

"No, I am fine, Cassandra," he said, looking crushed but sitting dry-eyed and straight. "I just don't have any ambition left. You took it all away. I should not have married you. A man can't very well get to the top when his wife is glued to the bottom. It just doesn't work."

Those quiet words made more noise than all the shouting. She couldn't let him disintegrate from the inside and go to pieces. So she gave in; she hired someone to care for her baby and went along with him, hating every minute of it. But every time she acquiesced, every time she overrode her better judgment by dancing and by having a cocktail, she suffered guilt and frustration.

Then came the final nail in the coffin of her marriage. Cassandra met a woman in the doctor's office who invited her to come to a home Bible study. Cassandra went, formed a friendship with Judy, and enjoyed the lesson. Over the weeks, she became so convicted of her reveling that she refused to go to another bash with Gil. God was not pleased with the wickedness.

Gil picked at her until he learned about the religious classes. Then he hit the ceiling and forbade her to return to Judy's house. "Unless you can conform to my way of life, you will leave," he vowed. "And I will have custody of my daughter. That's a guarantee. I know every lawyer in town." He became so abusive that Cassandra was terrified of him.

That year she met Thomas at a concert. She left town with him. Did she do the right thing? Maybe running away was not the answer.

Fourteen years ago. And she hadn't missed a night crying for her child. What would Gilla look like at seventeen? Would her hair still be blond? Would she still have dimples?

Thomas had been good to her. But how was she to foresee the stock market crash, the dissolving of his band, and their stranded, penniless existence on the cap rock? How was she to know that the bitter remorse would haunt her forever?

Thomas stood in the doorway. He had finished his work early. "Are you all right?"

She tried to hide her swollen eyes behind her hand.

"The same thing?" he asked, sympathy and care softening his voice. "Is it little Gilla?"

She nodded. "Oh, Thomas! Will it ever go away?"

"Not until you make contact with her. I will take you down to the pay box to let you make a telephone call. I can't bear to see you go on suffering year after year."

Cassandra shook her head slowly. "Not today, Thomas. I'm not ready yet. I'll call her on her eighteenth birthday. Then she will be of age, and Gil Carmichael can't interfere."

ELEVEN

DEATH NOTICE

Gil had a secret pastime. He liked to compose blurbs for the local newspaper while he sat in a bathtub of lukewarm water. He especially enjoyed the invention of blazing headlines that would make people gasp and stare and whisper. As he soaped and scrubbed, the startling captions thundered through his head. The imaginative sweep of his ideas was equaled only by his feeling of self-importance. From his earliest years he had booked frequent ego trips.

His bold proclamations might include: "Daughter of Prominent Businessman Wins Miss America Pageant," or "Big Government Contract Awarded Millionaire Gilbert Carmichael." All of the news items that he fabricated included himself, directly or indirectly.

And, of course, he had one favorite obituary that he never missed. G. Wilson Brumley. *G. Wilson Brumley, age 93, passed away on Monday. He was a longtime resident of McLennan County. There are no surviving relatives.*

As he sat in the tub this morning, he had been through the entire regimen. He dipped beneath the water and washed off the soapsuds. It was time to get out to lay another stone in his foundation of greatness. How many

MISTER B'S LAND

people envied him his position with the city? How many more would writhe with jealousy when he became wealthy?

He slicked back his hair with Vitalis to make it dark and glossy. Then he winked at himself in the mirror. He had put on some weight, but he was still alluring.

As he walked into the kitchen for his thermos of coffee, he switched the knob of the radio to the "on" position. It was set on a local station, booming out the seven o'clock news. A minute too late for the beginning, he caught the end of the story: . . . *was found dead at his residence southeast of the city.* Gil's breathing stopped. *He was ninety-three years of age and had no surviving family members. Graveside services will be tomorrow at 2 p.m.*

His breath came back in a whistle as the impact of the announcement hit him. Its unexpectedness brought a wave of exhilaration. G. Wilson Brumley, dead! This was the glorious day around which all his thoughts had revolved.

His mind began to make plans, sweeping away all the days he had existed on tenterhooks of anxiety and suspense. Suddenly, he burst out laughing, wildly, hilariously.

For ten years he had waited for this occasion. He had begun to think that old Brumley would live forever. These had been trying years for Gil, waiting for the old man to croak. Now it wouldn't be long until he had the land for his factories in the palm of his hand. Loading docks . . . a shipyard . . . wharves . . . piers . . . Ah, being a millionaire would be delicious! He hoped, wherever she was, that Cassandra would hear about this. And she would get her paws on none of it, for it was she who deserted him.

DEATH NOTICE

How long should he wait to lay his claim on the land? Three days? A week? He didn't wish to invoke public indignation with his lack of respect for the dead, but it might not hurt to get his word in immediately.

Gil changed his mind about going to his office. He opted, instead, to take his sketchbook out to the land to start taking a few notes. Trees that would need bulldozing. Banks sloped for ramps. Easement for roads. He could start the preliminaries, anyway.

Deep in mental diagramming, he frowned. The first course of action would be to get rid of the old shack and its contents. A bonfire would accomplish his purpose there.

In front of the property, he stopped his car, panned his eyes about, and gave a grunt of satisfaction. He let his fingers slide from the wheel. *A virtual gold mine lies within the span of your eyes, old boy,* he told himself. The thought ignited a burst of elation that reverberated through his body.

Leaving the car, he walked toward the old shack, a tacky thing, listing northeast. The windows were off square and the steps rotting. Mercilessly, the white sunlight showed the details of the jerry-built structure in its state of decay. It couldn't even be sold for scrap.

A blaze would consume it in ten minutes. He fingered the lighter in his pocket. Today? No one would know who did it, and who would care anyway? Everyone knew it was a firetrap waiting for a spark.

The outhouse would go, too. And if a few trees caught, so much the better. . . .

A twig snapped under Gil's feet, and the door of the cabin swung open. Gil gasped and jumped back. *Didn't the radio say—?*

MISTER B'S LAND

Jude Franklin stepped out, blinking against the glare of the sun.

"What are you doing here, young man?" Gil's words held the hint of a threat.

"I would ask you the same question, sir."

"I am here to check on my land."

"Your land?"

"You heard me." Gil said it distinctly, bearing a confidence that allowed no difficulties to stand in his way. "And I would advise you to leave my property at once."

Jude didn't flinch. "I would advise you to leave Mr. Brumley's property at once."

"Mr. Brumley is dead."

"Indeed he is. And the world is unfortunate for his going. There are few real men left. Mr. Brumley was a real man. But may I remind you, sir, that although he is departed, his land has not gone to probate. At this moment, his place is no more yours than it is mine."

"He had no heirs. I am a county tax assessor, and I have filed a petition to claim the land from the county."

If Gil could bluff, so could Jude. "I spent the last evening of Mr. Brumley's life with him, sir. He enjoyed a normal day with a clear mind. And he told me what he wished to become of his land. I am willing to state his wishes in court if need be."

Gil tried to corral his fear-fueled anger. "Unless you are kin to the deceased, your words will mean nothing in court. What are you doing in Mr. Brumley's house, anyway? Searching for a will?" His animosity flared, and like lightning around a rod, the atmosphere crackled with it.

"No, sir. As far as I know, Mr. Brumley left no will. The funeral director sent me here to try to find the date of Mr.

DEATH NOTICE

Brumley's birth. He reasoned that it might be recorded in the old man's Bible. I found it." Jude patted his shirt pocket. "But I haven't touched another thing, and I left the Bible on the stool right where it was."

"You should have taken it if you collect Bibles, because I plan to burn the shack and everything in it."

"Mr. Carmichael, if this house burns to the ground today or tomorrow or next week, you will be charged with arson and sent to prison." The words were emphatic, pithy. "Until the deed to the land is in your name, you have no right to plan or measure or destroy anything. And it would serve you well to remember that." Jude closed the door of the house behind him and walked off.

Arson. Prison. Phrases jumped out and grabbed Gil by his nerves. They had a strange ring as though they were not words at all but echoes. His head seemed to be hollow except for the sound they made. *Arson. Prison.* His fingers pulled away from the lighter. He repeated the words to himself until his mind cleared again. Then he turned and hurried back to his car.

Step one in his plan, to burn the house, had been quashed. Jude could ruin him, could set his doom bells ringing. What if lightning struck the shack? Jude would pin it on him.

But wait! What had Gilla said about Jude? Gil scratched around in his memory. Oh, yes. He had joined the military. In that case, he would only be home for a few days, and then he would be out of the way. He wouldn't be around to testify in a dead man's behalf.

There would be a bit more waiting. But this catch would be worth the extra time. One little setback was hardly noteworthy.

MISTER B'S LAND

The next day, Gil took himself to Mr. Brumley's funeral. His attendance would set well with the city; they would think him a mourning friend. Few others were there. The mailman. The milkman. The welfare caseworker. And Jude.

The mossy old parson, an uneducated fellow whom Gil decided had never seen the inside of a seminary, gave a rambling eulogy. It was something about the ground in which the dead rested being more sacred than the earth upon which the living walked because the pattern of yesterday was the promise of today and the pledge of tomorrow. It didn't make much sense to Gil, who'd had a nip before he came.

What he did understand, he disagreed with. No ground was more important than what he would soon gain. The thing to do was to look ahead, not backward. Thinking about the past was a sign of old age and decline.

After the minister had exhausted his words, two of the undertaker's men cranked the casket down into the hole, and it was over. The mourners left, but Gil hung back to talk with the mortician. Had Jude some connection with the dead man? he asked. No, the undertaker said, he was just a friend who had paid for the funeral expenses so that the old man could be buried where he wished rather than in a pauper's plot.

Why would Jude pay for the old man's funeral? Nobody was that generous unless there were advantages to be gained from his generosity. Gil was sure the young man had devious motives.

Jude Franklin. For the rest of the day, Gil skirted around the grievance of the young man's interference. If he hadn't been on the property, the shack would be gone and progress would have begun. If the bothersome boy hadn't gotten a leave from the army at the wrong time . . .

A sensation for which Gil had no name passed over him, pulling the warmth and excitement from him and replacing it with a dark, chilling shadow. It was only momentary, and not liking to acknowledge feelings that could not be captured and tabulated, he whisked it aside with vehemence. He would win! He would have his land!

As the finger of light from the waning moon passed slowly across the rumpled sheet and back toward the window sill that night, Gil reached beneath his bed for a box of pills hidden there and then gave himself to the murky territory of drugged sleep.

TWELVE

Nightmare

The summer was running out.

Gilla wanted to see Palo Duro Canyon, and Claudette had a cousin in Dumas that she wished to visit. So they decided to quarter in Amarillo for the last week of their junket. A downtown hotel offered the best accommodations.

The first night there, Gilla couldn't sleep. She lay in her bed, staring at the silver birds that preened on blue draperies. Was it that she regretted the curtain call of her leisure, or did she dread the inevitable conflict with her father?

In the recesses of her soul, a pulse of terror plagued her, a distress that resisted analysis as if something disastrous were in store for her. She couldn't shake the dark foreboding.

Amarillo slept. Why couldn't she? Her senses were alert, waiting, though for what she did not know. Outside, the evening had a luminescence, sourceless and disturbing. She let her mind wander with the noises of the night. A gaggle of geese heading south. A late motorcar on the street below going too fast, devouring the brick road. The tick of the Big Ben clock.

To what avail had been her journey? Her search for

truth, for life's meaning, had met with failure. Claudette was forbidden to discuss religion with her. She couldn't very well walk up to a stranger and start talking about God, could she?

Did all life's amenities end like this, like a set a tires, new and tough and full of interesting grooves at the first, then wearing thin as they rolled through time until they were ready to rupture? Gilla felt worn down; she had no more fight left in her.

She would go back to the same church with its white columns and stained-glass windows. To the same prayer books arranged neatly in the stack. To the same conscripted pew. To the wooden plate in which you placed your white envelopes with lavender crosses that held enough money to cover all your trespasses. To the same emptiness.

She pushed her legs over the side of the bed and stood at the window, seeing nothing. A peculiar loneliness beset her, steering her thoughts to someone she had reflected upon more and more of late: her mother. What was her mother like? Did she bear her favor? Why would a mother desert her only child? Why had she heard nothing from her mother in all these years? What would life have been like with a loving mother?

Gilla's father had sealed off the subject as taboo, offering short, bitter answers to any questions she asked about her mother. A perceptive youngster, she had learned early to avoid any discussion of the past. And tonight, the unknown came to haunt her.

She stayed at the window until her mind and body were numb with the biting air, and when at last she crawled back into bed and slept, it was in patches. Near

NIGHTMARE

morning, she had a ghastly dream in which something too horrible to happen was suddenly transpiring, and there was nothing she could do to stop it. From a wretched state between sleep and wakefulness, she became conscious in stages of gloom, fright, and then panic. At last, she lay wide awake, drenched with a clammy sweat.

When Claudette knocked on her door at nine o'clock, Gilla was shaking violently, clutching a blanket tightly to her body to form one more layer of protection over the icy core of her heart. "You are ill, Gilla," Claudette said. "We must get you to a doctor at once."

"N-n-no, Claudette," she shivered. "I had a b-b-bad dream." She covered her face with her hands and began to weep.

Claudette sat on the edge of the bed beside her, feeling her brow. "You have no fever," she pronounced. "Tell me about the dream."

"It was about my father." Another spasm of shaking gripped her.

"Dreams are fickle things, Gilla," reminded the chaperone. "They seldom have rhyme or reason."

"But it was so real! My father was leaning out the window of his office, four stories up, and—and he leaned out too far. He fell to the pavement below. I was screaming for someone to catch him, for someone to break his fall. I was running, but I couldn't get there fast enough—"

"Most folks have nightmares now and then. I have had them. You have been away from home all summer, and it is likely that you are missing your father. Why don't you ring him up on the telephone? He said that you could call collect anytime. I think hearing his voice would make you feel better." She patted Gilla's arm. "Get up and get dressed now, and we'll go to the lobby so that you can talk with him. He'll be glad to hear from you."

There was a fireplace at either end of the lobby, a crystal chandelier hanging from the ceiling in the middle, and a velvet-covered chair by the telephone table. Gilla asked the operator to connect her to Gil Carmichael's office with reversed charges.

She waited through clicks and beeps, tearfully relieved to hear her father's voice. It was clear and strong. He would gladly accept charges for a call from Gilla Carmichael, he told the operator.

"Gilla!" he boomed when the connection was complete. "Is everything all right? Where are you?"

Some of her misgivings leaked away. "I'm in Amarillo, and I was going to ask you the same question." She forced a shaky laugh.

"Why, I'm in fine form," he exuded. "I couldn't be better. In fact, I'm glad you called because I have some great news, and I didn't know where to reach you. Remember the old man who had the property out south of town?"

"Mr. Brumley?"

"Yes, G. Wilson Brumley. Well, we had his funeral yesterday."

"Oh, Dad, I'm sorry—"

"I'm not. One generation should move over for the next. He sat on that golden shelf long enough. Now it is my turn."

"Dad, I hope you won't cut down the trees and ruin the—"

"Now listen, baby. No sentimental stuff. I will make enough money off that land to buy you a tree-covered ranch anywhere in the world."

NIGHTMARE

"But, Dad, Mister B didn't want—"

"Mr. Brumley is dead and gone, and he will never know that his little old fishing hole has gone commercial. This is my lucky break. When you called, I was preparing to go to my lawyer to get the papers fixed up on that tract. By the time you get back next week, you will see different scenery south of town. You will be proud of your old paw! The city will sit up and take notice when I own the bank."

Gilla wanted to hear no more about it; she was sick inside. She changed the subject. "I miss my car."

"I've been driving it to keep the stiffness out of its joints."

"Did I get any mail?"

"Stacks of invitations. Your friend, Peggy Gossimer, is getting married next month. She wants you to be in her wedding. It will be at our church."

"Did I get any personal mail, Dad? Any letters?"

"You mean from that Judo fellow?" She could hear the derision in his voice. "No, but he came to the door asking for you last week."

Her heart jumped. "He did?"

"Yes, but I sent him packing. I knew that you had broken off with him, so I figured I would help you out. I told him that you had gone away and that you plan to be married." Gil's "heh, heh, heh" ripped Gilla apart like daggers.

"But, Dad! You lied to him!"

"It was just a joke, baby."

"Then you really didn't tell him that?"

"I really did. But I was only spoofing him so he wouldn't bother you anymore. Listen, Gilla, he isn't good enough for you—"

"Promise me you will call him today and will tell him the truth, Dad. Let me give you his number—"

"He has already left town. He was on a short leave from the army; he is shipping overseas. But listen, Gilla. There are plenty of others just waiting for you when you get here. There is the banker's son and—"

"I have to go, Dad. I am running up your bill."

"Who cares? We will soon have more money than we can spend, you and I."

"I'll see you in a few days."

She hung up, hurting to the lining of her soul. To dam a spurt of tears, she squeezed her eyelids tightly. Her father had told Judo a lie. A lie! Why had he done it? Judo would go overseas thinking she had betrayed him! And now the old man was dead, too, the old man who called her Miss Joseph. Where would she turn? And to think that her father was glad! It was too much.

When the first welter of anger subsided and a measure of coherent thought returned, she tried to find a reason, or at least an excuse, for her father's behavior. It was unforgivable.

"Is he all right?" Claudette asked.

"Who—? Oh, yes, he's fine," she answered. *But I'm not.*

THIRTEEN

A VISIT TO THE LAWYER

Gil carried his imported briefcase to give the impression of urgent matters. It was time for a talk with the lawyer.

Two things in Gil's possession were designed to make him look important: his ostrich case and his top hat. His hat was always glossy and well brushed, the lining boasting the label of one of the best hatters in the country. Tall, it enhanced his height by four or five inches, and its subtly curved brim introduced it unmistakably as the hat of a man of the world.

All his movements had a winner's tempo. The whole of his mannerism was largely a confidence trick; he had been playing it so long he had begun to believe it himself. He thought himself a great man. Every feature and every gesture were geared to generate an image of high achievement.

Inside the lawyer's office, he came eye to eye with the secretary, a hard-bitten woman in her fifties. "I must see Mr. Swaiz at once," he demanded.

She gave him an indifferent glance. "I'm sorry, Mr.—?"

"Carmichael. Gilbert Carmichael. It is imperative that I see the attorney today. He knows who I am, and he will be glad to adjust his schedule to accommodate me, I'm sure."

MISTER B'S LAND

"The lawyer is not in today."

Secretaries habitually covered for lawyers who were eating or sleeping or playing a game of chess. "My affairs are quite pressing. I suppose I will be obliged to find another lawyer. This case would mean a lot of money—"

"As you will, Mr. Carmichael. I repeat, my boss is not in today."

"When will he be back?"

"The day after tomorrow."

"Where is he? I will find him." Office workers could be immovably stubborn. Women who thought they owned a place should be fired.

"I think that is none of your business, sir. If you wish to see Mr. Swaiz, you may return later. Thank you, and I will tell him that you came by."

Gil's chest tightened in the mixture of anger and frustration that always came over him when he met a glitch in his plans. He had hoped to persuade the lawyer to go with him to estimate the land's value. His mood swung like a weathercock in a change of wind, and he stalked out, batting the air with disgraceful words for the woman who was doing her job.

The stifling heat of August's brassy sky pressed down on Gil's black headgear. He hurried back to the office so he would be free to remove his hat. Up the stairs and down the hall, he was surprised to find a small sign fastened to his door. Then he remembered that he had put it there himself to notify customers he was out on business for the day. Angry with himself for forgetting—and a little disturbed at his forgetfulness—he unlocked the office door with his key.

In the doorway he paused, looking around the cramped

A VISIT TO THE LAWYER

little room and the old desk littered with papers. He scowled at a mote-filled beam of slanting sun pointing like an accusing finger to the stack of tax notices he had neglected to mail this morning. However, it was only a minute segment of his brain that registered the oversight. This occurrence happened to him often, as it was happening now, when he had drunk too heavily the night before. Was he starting to lose a deeper stream of consciousness that kept him aware of his duties?

Nor did Gil go to work the next day. Until he had an opportunity to talk with Mr. Swaiz, he had no incentive, no ambition to set his mind to other action. What were a couple more days when he would soon be resigning the piddling city job anyway?

Those two days passed in a red blur. He didn't remember going to bed or getting up, but he did manage to get back to Mr. Swaiz's office on the appointed day.

The attorney greeted him a bit stiffly, professionally. "Mr. Carmichael," he nodded. "My secretary informed me that you wished to speak with me. I am at your service."

"Yes," Gil lowered himself into a chair in front of the lawyer's desk and turned his hat to where the label could be seen. "I've come to draw up a deed on some property I wish to purchase."

"How may I help? Does the abstract need to be brought up to date?"

"I don't know. The land I want belonged to a G. Wilson Brumley, recently deceased. It is south and east of town. On the river. I want it for commercial purposes. A manufacturing plant. Munitions. For the government."

"And you wish me to check to see if the area is zoned for such a project?"

MISTER B'S LAND

"No, I want it transferred to my name."

"I am ill supplied with the details of the man's death. Very desirable property, that. You are an heir of Mr. Brumley, then?"

"Oh, no. Mr. Brumley had no heirs. So if you will help me with the transfer of deed, I would like to get immediate possession. It is imperative that I start cleaning up the place this week. The old shack will be the first to go—"

"Not so fast, Mr. Carmichael. I'm afraid we have a little legal problem here. If there were no heirs listed—and no written will—there will be a six-month waiting period before the land can be put up for public auction by the county. Notices must be posted in several newspapers around the country in the event that a survivor has been inadvertently overlooked."

"But—"

"Also, if perchance Mr. Brumley left any indebtedness behind, those creditors must have an opportunity to come forward in that time period."

"But surely you can break that stipulation," Gil winked, "for a nice price."

Mr. Swaiz smiled. "I wouldn't break it for any price, sir. It is a good law. And fair. If it were my property or yours, we would want such protection."

"But I need to start to work on the factories. With the clouds of war— You see, I'm doing it for the good of our country."

"Your chances of acquiring the land will be as good as the next, depending on your financial ability to outbid your competitors. An auction will be held on the courthouse steps. You can watch the newspaper for a public

A VISIT TO THE LAWYER

notice, or my secretary will send you a written notice. For a prepaid fee, of course."

Gil's pockets were empty. "Will it be agreeable for me to go out to look around a bit?" he asked. "I'd like to get an estimate of the property's dimensions."

"A legal description can be found in the county clerk's office. For that matter, you should have a copy of the dimensions in your tax files."

Gil's cheery comeback was faked. "It is always easier to measure with the eye and in person," he said.

"That wouldn't be advisable, Mr. Carmichael. In the event that an anonymous heir should abruptly show up and find you on the place, he or she could have you penalized for trespassing. I'd say bide your time with the rest. There is no need to get antsy; land is stationary. It isn't going to wander off. Good day, sir."

Gil took his hat and left. "I'll get the land," he swore under his breath, refusing to entertain the possibility of any other outcome.

But how could he stave off the hounds of overextended credit that nipped at his heels this moment? He took out his handkerchief and mopped his brow. A matter of minutes ago, there had been no problem on the horizon of his life. Now he would have to figure a new scheme to keep the finance company from repossessing Gilla's car, the electric company from disconnecting his utilities, and the bank from foreclosing on his home. How would he gather the funds to pay for Gilla's college tuition?

His income had dwindled to a trickle while he waited for his dream to become reality, a dream that had moved six months into the future—thanks to an idiotic law. *The only function is to endure,* he reminded himself. *Say it*

MISTER B'S LAND

three times, and it will come true. Endure. Endure. Endure.

Characteristically, he began to lay plans. *Gilla will come home next week. I will quit drinking. That will save money. Gilla will fall in love with the banker's son; it will be love at first sight. That development will give me an inroad to the banking institution, into more borrowing power. . . .*

There was nothing like a glamorous daughter to fill her father's heart with hope. Ah, and he would repay her. When he was filthy rich, he would throw marvelous parties in her honor. Knights in shining armor would appear as if by magic to swim and to dance with her. She would live a fairy-tale life. . . .

Gilla. His beautiful Gilla. What surprise could he have waiting for her when she came home? A sequined evening gown? Pearl earrings? An appointment with the salon to have her hair bobbed and styled for college?

Humming, he started for home.

FOURTEEN

DAWN

They had seen the canyon, its colors dry and burnt like the colors of pottery. Gilla liked the park composed of stilted formations, sloping perilously down to the bed of the canyon. Dark mesas walled off the sky, their caliche and sandstone smoldering in the sun. Wherever a little soil covered the ravine's floor, ocotillo flowers struggled to seize the ground.

But Claudette insisted that the chief feature of the high plains was the air—alive, waving, and shining like running water, mirroring objects, creating mirages. Here, she said, she could breathe freely, inhale with an ease arrogantly ahead of anything born in the southern part of the state.

The only thing yet on schedule was Claudette's visit to her cousin in Dumas, an event she planned for Saturday after breakfast. She invited Gilla to go with her, but Gilla declined, saying she wanted to enjoy some quiet time before her return to a full schedule of school.

"Are you sure that you will be okay without me, Gilla?" Claudette quizzed. "I didn't ask your father if I might have a day off."

"Please go. I want a day to myself, Claudette. Too much 'Sneezing' isn't good for me," teased Gilla. They both laughed.

MISTER B'S LAND

Claudette took a bus to Amarillo's northern neighbor, and Gilla went to her room. She reread the story of Joseph, wiping tears both for the emotional impact of Joseph's history and for the dear old gentleman who had acquainted her with him. She noted that Joseph's father spent seventeen years with his son before their separation and seventeen years afterward. God, she thought, had a special way with numbers.

She then read some verses in the New Testament that only intensified her yearning for spiritual enlightenment. Finally, she laid aside her Bible and wept bitterly. *God, I know that I am missing some great truth in Your Word. There must be a change in my life, but I don't know how to accomplish it. I have a craving inside to really know You. . . .*

The wind from the open window ruffled the pages of the Bible, turning them and losing her place. Her reddened eyes fell upon a verse in Matthew: *Blessed are they which do hunger and thirst after righteousness: for they shall be filled.* The verse leaped out, magnified. Those fifteen words shone as a beacon through the fog. Suddenly she understood. Finding God would not be a matter of intellect but of faith, a belief that He would reveal Himself to her. How, she did not yet know, but He would do it. *God, please let me find You before I go home!* her heart cried. *I am hungry and thirsty.*

She slept through the larger portion of the afternoon, inertia claiming her drained spirit. When she awoke, her body called for food.

The tea room adjoined an oblong dining area where a group of people had gathered for a time of fellowship. Feeling no particular rush, Gilla ate her sandwich slowly, one ear attuned to the party next door. They seemed a joyous group, infected with cheer.

When she had finished her repast, she got up to leave. A lovely sound of music filled the air, followed by voices in unison. And such singing! She moved toward the open door, pulled by some magnet of the heart. *Amazing grace, how sweet the sound, that saved a wretch like me. . . .*

Excitement like a current charged through her. These folks sang as though they lived their song! She did not realize that her feet had taken her to the room's entryway and that she was peeking in. Some of the people clapped their hands, some patted their feet, while others closed their eyes as if in a state of rapture.

A woman in a wheelchair, sitting near the door, beckoned to Gilla. "Please join us, dear," she whispered, patting the chair beside her. "You can sit here with me."

"But I was not invited to the party," Gilla said.

"Everyone is invited," the woman smiled.

Gilla sat down, enchanted by the moving songs and by the man who played the ebony piano with such fervor. Although she did not know the words of the hymns, her soul joined in the melody. She was being lifted higher and higher, leaving behind earth's cares, wanting to laugh and to cry at the same time. What was happening to her? Whatever it was, it was good. And real. And right.

After the singing, there were testimonies. One and then another of the group told what God had done for them. Gilla strained to catch every sentence, every word.

The crippled lady beside her related how her best friend became a Christian and introduced her to salvation's plan. Many and hard had been her burdens, she said, but God's love had sustained her. She asked prayer for her daughter that she might be saved.

A man told of being delivered from an addiction to alcohol. Another, an elderly fellow, talked about heaven and his great desire to go there where his beloved wife had gone. He reminded Gilla of Mr. Brumley.

Gilla hoped that they might go on talking for a long while. She felt that she was on the brink of some wonderful revelation and sat eagerly waiting for that moment to arrive. Yet it didn't come.

Then it was over, and Gilla experienced a great letdown. She would travel back to her hometown and never see these people again, foundering her chance to learn what made them so happy.

The woman beside her was speaking. "Have you met the Master, dear?"

"You mean the man who played the piano?" asked Gilla.

"No, dear. I'm talking about the Master of all ages. Jesus. Have you been filled with His Spirit?"

Filled. The Scripture in Matthew flashed back to Gilla. *Blessed are they which do hunger and thirst after righteousness: for they shall be filled.* Was this the filling of which the verse spoke? His Spirit?

"No," Gilla answered honestly. "But I would like very much to be filled."

"Oh, then you shall be, dear."

Gilla thought that she had never seen a lovelier face, a face illuminated with a radiant glow. How could a woman who could not walk be happy? An intangible and wonderful empathy reached out from the woman's smiling eyes and touched Gilla with its powerful appeal. Here was a lady who would understand one's heartaches, one's confusion. Gilla wished that she might spend time talking with her.

As if the woman read Gilla's mind, she began to talk about the love of Jesus. About His sacrifice for her sins and His willingness to make her His child. Hungrily, Gilla listened, drinking in every syllable. Surely God was preparing her for His gift.

"And do you live here?" the woman asked.

"No, ma'am, I'm only passing through."

Disappointment was written in the woman's expression. "I am sorry to hear that. We are holding a church service in our home tomorrow, and I wish that you could be there."

"I won't be leaving until Monday."

The man who played the piano had joined them. "In that case, would you like to worship with us in the morning?" He was tall and slim with slightly rounded shoulders.

"I would like it very much," Gilla heard herself say. "If you will tell me how to get there, I will hire a cab."

"Oh, by no means!" objected the man. "I will come for you. Is nine-thirty agreeable?"

"Yes," Gilla said. "And my traveling companion may come with me."

"Good! Good!" he cheered. "The more the merrier! And by the way, my name is Mr. McLellan, and this is Dawn McLellan."

"That should be easy enough to remember," Gilla smiled. "I live in McLennan County."

Dawn's eyes lighted; they were brilliantly blue and mesmerizing. "You do? My best friend, the one of whom I spoke this evening, lived in McLennan County. Her name was Judy. Judy Franklin. She was a wonderful Christian. But Judy has been dead for several years now. God took her on home. She left behind a little boy named Jude."

Jude. Jude Franklin. Could it be?

"I know a Jude Franklin. He is my best friend."

"Truly? What a coincidence."

"His friends call him Judo."

"Exactly!" She clapped her hands together. "Judy started calling him that when he was a baby. Tell me, where is Judy's son now?"

"He is in the army."

"Oh, dear! And with the shadow of war hanging over our heads! We certainly must pray that the Lord will keep him safe and that I shall see him again to tell him what a lovely mother he had. She won me to God. Now isn't it a small world?"

Gilla wanted to wrap her arms around Dawn McLellan, a woman who had known Judo and his mother. Instead, she reached out and touched Dawn's hand. "I'm glad you told me."

"I had better take you home now, Dawn," Mr. McLellan insisted. "I know that you must be tired."

"Truly, I feel wonderful," Dawn beamed.

"You can visit more tomorrow."

He pushed the chair from the room as Dawn called back, "Read the second chapter of Acts tonight, dear. That wonderful Holy Ghost experience is for all of us. Peter will give you the requirements."

When they had gone, their departure left an extraordinary vacuum; Gilla's sun had been lost behind a cloud. She felt herself sinking once more into her familiar morass of emptiness. The delightful evening and the blissful release it brought fled.

Back in her hotel room, Gilla fell prey to loneliness such as she had never encountered before.

FIFTEEN

Surprise Discovery

Claudette came in late from Dumas; Gilla was still up reading the Book of Acts. "I'm sorry to be so tardy, Gilla," Claudette apologized. "Patsy and I were reliving our childhood days, and we almost lived too long! I scarcely got to the bus station to catch the last coach out."

"You should have just stayed on until tomorrow."

"Naw, we had been in our second childhood long enough," she laughed.

She declined Gilla's invitation to attend church. "I had best not go," she excused. "Gilbert Carmichael might construe my going with you as 'encouraging a religious notion,' and that was interdicted in my employment. Anyway, I'd as soon sleep here as in church. Most church services put me into a terrible drowse."

"These people would keep you awake," promised Gilla. "They are lively."

Claudette arched her penciled brows. "Miz Sneeze will stay and snooze."

That night a fall-announcing mist hung heavy outside, and Gilla slept intensely, free of dreams. She had set her alarm, but she failed to wind it. It was five minutes before nine when she awoke. Mr. McLellan would be by for her in half an hour!

MISTER B'S LAND

Scurrying about in a frenzy of haste, she clapped her hat on her head, jabbing hatpins into place. With a dive into the wardrobe, she fished out her gloves and a purse. Then casting one last look at her unmade bed, she ran to the lobby. This was one meeting she couldn't miss!

Mr. McLellan was waiting for her. His worn, shapeless suit reminded Gilla of the lining of a suitcase. He led the way to his car, a very ancient one but clean, offering no excuses for its threadbare interior. "Your traveling friend didn't wish to come?" he asked. "Miss—?"

"Claudette. No, sir. She got in very late from a visit with her cousin and is still sleeping. She isn't very—religious."

"Dawn would have loved to come along," he mentioned, "but getting her in and out of a vehicle takes time. And she wanted to put on lunch for anyone who would stay to eat with us."

"She had polio?"

"No, she has a rare form of arthritis that renders her bones quite breakable. She must never put her weight on her feet or legs."

"Then she is in a great deal of pain?"

"Actually, she has no physical pain. We consider that a miracle."

"She is a beautiful lady."

"That she is. And brave. Sometimes a person comes to great strength through trials and weakness and ailments. I think this has happened to Dawn."

The McLellans' home was north of town, a flat-roofed adobe building with a somewhat ramshackle appearance. "This is the home God has provided for Dawn and me, and we are thankful for it," the man said.

SURPRISE DISCOVERY

Inside, the floor was covered with cracked linoleum. Apparently someone was in the process of resurfacing the walls but had gotten only as far as scraping off the old plaster. The living room was long and narrow with a heater situated at one end, some of its grates missing. A collection of old hymnbooks rested in a makeshift bookcase, and a battered piano was shoved against the wall to make room for the haphazard profusion of mismatched chairs. The whole place smelled of homemade soap and fresh air.

Dawn McLellan had nestled her wheelchair beside a dilapidated brown leather recliner. When Gilla entered, she nodded to the chair, her face shining. "Right here, dear. Sit by me. You are alone? Your friend didn't—?"

"Claudette. No, she didn't come."

"And did you read the Acts?"

"I did."

"Good. Your salvation is coming. God has given me that blessed assurance." She squeezed Gilla's hand, and Gilla felt a thrill of anticipation.

"I hope so. I am ready."

The small congregation gathered, along with a parson. The service began with each participant voicing his needs aloud. Gilla sat quietly. "And our young visitor wants the gift of the Holy Ghost," Dawn supplied for Gilla.

After a rousing prayer, Mr. McLellan distributed the old hymnals. Gilla was glad, for now she could follow the singing. She especially liked "Savior, Like a Shepherd Lead Me."

When the minister read his opening text, Gilla caught her breath. *Blessed are they which do hunger and thirst after righteousness: for they shall be filled.* That was her verse, her promise! She was hungry. She was thirsty. She was ready for the fruition of her promise.

At the end of his message, the preacher asked those who wished to be filled to come forward and kneel. Gilla rose from her chair and pressed her way to the front. She remembered little else until a bubbling joy swept her away in its wake. It flowed from inside, and the language that she spoke was not her own. No one had prepared her for such ecstasy! No one had said, "What you are, you will no longer be; all that you could not be, now you are." No one had described the feeling of cleanliness, of pure love.

Oh, there would be problems to surmount—especially where her father was concerned—but now she had an individual relationship with God. He dwelt within, and He would be her guide.

She ran to Dawn and flung her arms about her. "Oh, Mrs. McLellan, I have been filled!" she cried. "I feel as if I might burst with gladness!" She wept on the woman's neck.

When the service was dismissed, Dawn welcomed everyone to stay to share a meal with them. She had made a pot of soup. However, one and then another had reasons for departing. "But you will eat with us, won't you, Claudette?" she asked Gilla.

Gilla opened her mouth to decline, but seeing Dawn's imploring eyes, she said yes instead. Now why did she do that? Claudette would wonder what was keeping her. And Mrs. McLellan thought Gilla's name was Claudette! Things were getting in a mix, but she was too happy to care. Here in this poor and humble home was the first true contentment she had ever known, and she wasn't eager to leave it.

Dawn rolled herself to the kitchen, amazing Gilla with her proficiency in the serving of a meal. Gilla helped with

SURPRISE DISCOVERY

small tasks. Mr. McLellan shared in the talk during the meal, and Gilla felt quite at ease. What mattered that the bowls were chipped and the spoons a cheap pewter? A generous spirit found residence here.

When the meal ended, Dawn said, "We would like to keep you forever, Claudette, and we will miss you when you are gone, but when you are ready, Mr. McLellan will drive you back to your hotel."

"If you will give me time to add a quart of motor oil, please." Mr. McLellan darted out.

"I would like your address so that we can correspond," Dawn requested. "You are a part of our Christian family now. There is little I can do while Mr. McLellan is at work but read and write. It will be a pleasure to hear from someone who knows Judy Franklin's son."

Gilla pulled a note sheet from her purse, wrote her name and address, folded the paper, and handed it to Dawn. "My name isn't Claudette," she explained. "That is my chaperone's name. I am sorry you misunderstood. My name is Gilla."

"Gilla?" A dismayed look spread across Dawn's face.

"Gilla Carmichael."

"Oh!" Dawn's hands fluttered to her throat, and the color drained from her face.

"Since you knew the Franklins, did you perhaps know my father? Gilbert Carmichael?"

"Gil—? I—knew him—well." The words staggered out, stopping and starting, bumping against each other.

"And would you have met my mother, Cassandra Carmichael? I really don't remember much about her. She . . . left us . . . when I was three."

Dawn nodded faintly, and it was obvious to Gilla that

she was too overcome with emotion to speak. She seemed to be choking. This woman must know some truth about her mother that Gilla did not know. Her father had hidden a dark secret from her. Was her mother dead? Abducted? Murdered?

Mr. McLellan came in, and seeing Dawn sway, he rushed to her. "What is the matter, Dawn? Are you all right?" He turned to Gilla. "Get a wet towel. Dawn is near collapse; she is ill."

Dawn shook her head almost imperceptibly, her eyes never leaving Gilla's face. "Thomas!" she whispered. "This is little Gilla." Then to Gilla, weeping, "I am Cassandra Dawn Carmichael. I am your mother. Oh, my precious little Gilla! How I have prayed for this day—"

"She is overwrought," Mr. McLellan said. "I must put her to bed. She thinks that you are her daughter, Gilla Carmichael, and—"

"I am Gilla Carmichael."

"But I thought you were Claudette. You are—? There must be some mistake. Dawn's husband was Gilbert Carmichael."

"He is my father."

"And to think, Thomas, God brought my daughter to our house for her meeting with Him. It is too wonderful!" She reached for Gilla's trembling hand and kissed it. "Please do not leave, Gilla, until we have time for a long talk."

"If your husband can take a note to Claudette for me so that she won't worry . . ." Gilla couldn't leave until she had some answers.

"Yes, Thomas will take your note, dearest. But Thomas isn't my husband; he is my brother. Your father is still my husband."

SIXTEEN

A NEW PURPOSE

"There are hundreds of questions I want to ask, Mother," Gilla said, enjoying the gratifying sound of the endearment. She sat at her mother's feet with her head on Cassandra's knees while her mother stroked her hair.

"And there are hundreds of questions I will be glad to answer," responded Cassandra. "For years I have wanted you to know why I left. Each time I mailed your birthday card, I prayed you would contact me."

"My birthday card? I didn't get a birthday card."

"There have been fourteen of them, all addressed to you. Do you and your father still live at the same location on Maple Street?"

"Yes. I am sorry, Mother. I guess the cards were intercepted."

"I was afraid that might happen. I planned to try to reach you by phone next year on your eighteenth birthday when you would no longer be a minor. We have no telephone, but Thomas said he would take me to a pay box."

"If it isn't too painful, tell me everything from the beginning. Dad has told me nothing. The mention of you makes him angry. He destroyed all your pictures, and my imagination had no brush with which to paint a mother for myself. I wondered if you were even alive."

"I don't want to speak ill of your father, dear. I want you to honor him. That is the Bible's command. I pray for his salvation every day. He is a man who must be delivered from his passion and pride."

"But I must know the truth, Mother. Please, don't spare me."

"Thomas and I, as well as an older brother, were adopted out to separate families when I was yet in grammar school. Our father worked in the coal mines and died of what they called the 'black spit.' Our mother grieved herself to death.

"My parents loved God; He was at the center of their lives. Thank God, I had a small golden age before my parents died—only ten years—a brief span of dream days that made my growing up years bearable.

"The family who adopted me moved to Texas. They had no time for God, and I was not permitted to attend church. I was kept busy every day of the week.

"Your father and I met in a cotton patch when I was sixteen and he twenty-two. Both of us had our roots in poverty.

"I loved Gilbert Carmichael then, and I still love Gilbert Carmichael. His actions are not his own but the greed within him. I wanted to be the best wife in the world, to make him ultimately happy. I asked nothing more than what little he could provide.

"But Gil was ambitious, which wouldn't have been bad had he kept his priorities straight. Money became his lust, and he began to drink socially. To move up in the world, he felt a need to prove himself as a social monarch. He insisted that I join him in the partying, the drinking, the dancing."

A NEW PURPOSE

Gilla listened with rapt attention as her mother spilled the heartaches Gil's selfishness had created.

"The stress became overwhelming. My nerves were near deterioration, my legs began to ache, and my appetite fled. That is when I went to the doctor, and he discovered the disease. Within six months, he said, I would be a cripple, bound to a wheelchair for the rest of my life.

"I did not tell Gil. I feared that since I would prove a burden to him, both physically and financially, he would divorce me and would get custody of you. He knew every lawyer in town, and he knew how to make his money talk. He once threatened me. He said if I tried to leave, taking you, that I would pay with my life. I believed him.

"Moreover, my prognosis gave me little hope that I could care for you or support you. So torn was I that I thought my heart would break. Yet I felt God would protect you while He sustained me.

"My brother came through with a traveling orchestra. He recognized me even though we hadn't seen each other in years. When I told him my dilemma, he offered to take me with him and to provide for me. It seemed the best solution. The only solution.

"Things went fairly well for Thomas until the Great Depression hit in 1929. Then no one had money to hire or to hear a group of musicians. He lost his entire band. We were stranded right here in Amarillo. Thomas went to work in the stockyard, and we managed to buy this place. It isn't much, but it has sheltered us from rain and cold.

"Most of Thomas's money has gone to buy my medication, which is very costly." Cassandra exhaled a small sigh. "I suppose I have managed all my life to be a burden to someone."

"Is your disease life threatening?" asked Gilla.

"No. Only crippling. But I have no pain. In my body, that is. My heart has known great agony. But now . . . now that I have seen you . . . and know that you are in God's family, my heart can rest. I can sleep tonight without the salt of tears."

"Don't worry, Mother. I will come to see you often. Dad has done well financially. He bought me a nice little roadster for my birthday this year, and I will come on holidays."

"Oh, my dear, sweet daughter! Your visits will give me something to look forward to, to live for! How could I be so blessed?"

"Dad may object to my visits, but he cannot stop me when I am eighteen."

"Gilla, I think you should not tell your father about our meeting until you are of age. I am a bit frightened as to the tactics he might employ to keep us apart. I'm not saying you should be dishonest if he asks—"

"He often gets the mail. He will know right away that we are corresponding."

"Oh, that could pose a problem. Would it be wrong if I use an assumed name to write to you? Would it be unjust to tell him that the letters are from someone you met on vacation?"

"I don't feel in my heart that it would be wrong. Or—" Gilla snapped her fingers. "I can get a box number at the post office and let you know about it so you can address the letters there."

"That's a better idea. Now, tell me about you and Judo. Is there any romance involved? Where did you meet him?"

A NEW PURPOSE

"Judo went to our church. I met him at a youth fellowship. He was different from any other young man of my acquaintance. Judo was real, great hearted. The first time he came to see me, he brought the loveliest bouquet of flowers that he had picked himself. He said God grew them, not some stuffy hothouse, and therefore they bore God's own smile. Dad became angry and threw them away."

"But why?"

"He said if a young man couldn't buy expensive flowers from the florist, I should not accept 'weeds.' Then Judo began questioning our formalized religion; worship should be spontaneous. Our gratitude should come from the heart, he said."

"Oh, Judy would be so glad to know! That sounds just like something she would say."

"Judo and I understood each other well and had long talks. About the same time, I met an old gentleman who started me reading the Bible. I like the story of Joseph the best, so he nicknamed me Miss Joseph. Dad blamed Judo for the changes in me and banned my seeing him again.

"My heart was broken, and I feared I would challenge Dad's command. However, before the showdown came, Judo joined the army and went away. He said that he would write to me. I liked him very much—no, I loved him—and I thought the feeling was mutual, but I heard not a word from him—" Gilla stopped abruptly, struck by a painful thought. "But his letters may have been intercepted, too." She put her hands over her face.

"Don't worry, dear. God will right every wrong."

"When I talked with Dad this week by telephone, he said Judo had called on me during his furlough. Dad told him a . . . a falsehood. He said that I was engaged to be married to someone else. And Judo will have to go overseas thinking that I have been untrue to him!"

"God can take care of that, too. What changes were you speaking of, Gilla, when you said Gil blamed Judo for them?"

"Dad had a habit of entering me into beauty contests. I didn't feel comfortable presenting my body to the earthly judges after I read Paul's admonition to present my body a living sacrifice unto God. I won several beauty titles and made Dad proud. But my heart wasn't in the last one, and I lost.

"That is why Dad sent me on this trip: to get my mind off religion."

"And you did!" Cassandra rejoiced. "You forgot religion and got salvation."

"Dad will not be happy about that either."

"What are your plans when you return. Is it tomorrow?"

"Yes. I will be enrolling in Baylor University this fall. Dad wants me to become a certified public accountant so I may work for his business."

"What is his business now?"

"He works for the city as a tax assessor, but he has his plans tied to a giant manufacturing and shipping complex on the river. For months, he has been waiting for the ninety-three-year-old owner of a prime piece of property to die so he can purchase the place. The old fellow died this past week, leaving no heirs. He had a beautiful plot, untouched by modernism, and it was his wishes that it be left untainted, free from developments. I fished there myself, and it grieves me to see it disturbed. But Dad will

A NEW PURPOSE

go to any means to turn it into a booming business district. A location is all that stands between him and vast money. He says that he will be a millionaire almost overnight."

"Ah, Gilla. Money is not Gil's answer. He will only lust for more. His soul is crying for attention."

"I hope that I may lead him to God."

"I will pray."

The end of Gilla's visit loomed. How could she say good-bye to a mother she had just discovered? Both were silent, dreading the parting.

Suddenly, Gilla reached for her mother's hand. "I—I cannot leave you, Mother. I will stay. Claudette can go home alone. I will call Dad."

"No, Gilla. You must not stay. You are a minor, and your father still has legal power over you. Someday, but not yet. It is not God's will. Thomas cannot support us both, and you must get your education. It is very important."

"You are right, Mother, but when I am graduated from college, I will make very good wages. Would you consider coming to live with me?"

"Sweet Gilla, I cannot do that. I was a burden to my adoptive parents. I was a burden to Gilbert Carmichael. I have been a burden to Thomas McLellan. I will not be a burden to you."

"Please, listen, Mother. You will not be a burden to me. You will be a joy, a spiritual counselor, a friend, and a companion. I have been very lonely."

"What about this Claudette?"

"Dad hired her to travel with me; that's all. She is an agnostic and cares nothing for my friendship. Another job will call, and she'll forget me. I need you. I'd like to take you with me right now, but I would have no way to care for you while I am in school. Oh, I am eager to get home and have my education behind me as quickly as possible so that I may have you with me the sooner!"

Cassandra wiped away the flood of tears and smiled. "I can identify with Joseph's father who said, 'It is enough.' I have seen my lovely daughter, have seen God fill her with His Spirit, and come what may, I will magnify the Lord for this great miracle!"

My life now has purpose. I have found myself, my mother, and my God, Gilla thought, and when she looked up, she decided that an angel couldn't have a fairer smile or a more comely face than the one before her.

SEVENTEEN

Home Again

"Do you feel well, Gilla?" Claudette looked at Gilla strangely when she came in. "Your face is flushed. You haven't a fever, have you?"

"Oh, I feel marvelous, Claudette," Gilla assured. "I have never felt better in my life!"

How could she explain that the great light which blinded Paul on the road to Damascus had shone down on her seeking soul? How could she convey the heavenly joy of finding herself, her mother, and her God all in one day? Only a spiritual mind could comprehend such rapture, and Claudette hadn't a spiritual mind.

"If this has anything to do with religion, you are to inform your father that I did not promote it or approve of it," Claudette warned. "I will not be blamed for anything you have gotten yourself into concerning church."

"You have absolutely nothing to worry about, Claudette. You will not be held accountable for anything I experienced today."

"And what did you experience?"

"I've been born again."

Claudette pounded her forehead with her hand. "Poor, poor Gilbert Carmichael!"

The trip home was laden with tension. Claudette's agitation burgeoned. Anger often replaced the tempered geniality of her countenance, the effect of which was rather like the rolling of a dark thundercloud.

The friction, Gilla concluded, could be blamed on a clash of spirits. "I fear, Gilla Carmichael, that your father wasted his time and money on you," Claudette lamented. "Don't you know there will be plenty of years in your dotage to be a stick-in-the-mud fanatic without wasting your youth with your nose stuck in a Bible? Take my advice to enjoy life."

"I am enjoying life, Claudette. To the fullest. I have never enjoyed it more. If I were any happier, I would simply explode. I wish that everyone, including you, could share my joy."

"Hmph," she snorted. "I wouldn't call listening to some stodgy parson a joy. In fact, I haven't seen you befriend any excitement on this whole trip!"

"But I found what I was looking for."

"And just what, may I ask, were you looking for?"

"Peace in my heart."

After that short dialogue, the trip was accomplished in silence. When they reached their destination, it was clear that Claudette was anxious to part ways with her charge. She gathered her gear, hailed a taxi, and went directly home from the train depot, hardly giving Gilla a fare-thee-well.

Gilla looked about for her father. He had said he would meet her, but he was not there. He must have been delayed.

"Miss Carmichael!" Gilla's head snapped around at the sound of her name. A tanned, boyish face grinned down at her. Coal black hair was parted in the middle, but on one side a lock fell in a little curl over his forehead. His careless manner betrayed indolence, boredom, and conceit. A narrow-brimmed fedora sat jauntily on the back of his head. She guessed him to be a year or two older than she was.

"I am Devon Fitzwaren, the banker's son. Your father sent me for you. He is not feeling well."

A pang of alarm gripped Gilla. "Is he—quite ill?"

Devon flicked an eyelid flirtatiously. "I think he just wanted me to meet you. He has been telling me all about his gorgeous daughter. He showed me some of the clippings of the beauty contests you have won. I especially liked the picture of you in the bathing suit. I rather expected a—a siren, but really, you look quite—" he stumbled for a word, "harmless."

"Thank you."

"You have been traveling, of course, and must be tired. One mustn't judge a bewitching woman at the end of a day's journey on a rattletrap of a train."

"I feel fine."

"Your father says you are a great dancer. In fact, he has arranged for us a date to the dance at the country club Saturday night. You'll have all week to rest. There will be live entertainment. The minimum age is eighteen, and your father tells me you aren't there yet, but we can tell them that you are." He looked her over. "You'll pass for an adult.

"But perhaps I shouldn't have told you about the dance. Mr. Carmichael may have planned it as a surprise."

"Really, I must beg to be excused," Gilla said sweetly. "I will be getting ready to enter the university. There will be washing and ironing—"

Devon shrugged. "It was your father's idea and his dough, not mine."

As they pulled to the curb in front of Gilla's house, she

noticed that her car was not in the driveway. She rushed through the front door to find her father slumped on the couch with an ice pack on his head. His prostrate figure reminded her of a great oak that had fallen one stormy day when she was a little girl. She had cried for it. With time, its huge trunk rotted, sinking closer to the earth, gradually melting into the soil. The realization that something similar was happening to her father beset Gilla as she looked at him. She was amazed to see how he had crumbled in the short weeks of her absence.

"Are you ill, Dad?" she asked.

He looked at her through bloodshot eyes. "Just a beastly headache, Gilla. It's good to have you home."

"Let me get my bags to my room, and I'll fix you some supper."

"Sounds good."

She rushed to unpack and then went to the kitchen. An empty whiskey bottle sat on the table, and when she moved to drop a can into the garbage, she took note that it was filled with other bottles. Her father had been drinking heavily.

During the meal, Gilla brought up the subject of Gil's drinking. "I am worried that you are damaging your health," she cautioned.

"My weakness." He blinked and stared at her. "Every man has a weakness, or we would be sprouting wings and plucking harps. But now that you are home, I will drink no more."

"Where is my car? I didn't see it in the driveway."

"It is in the shop."

Gilla noticed that he would not look at her. "Did you . . . wreck it?"

HOME AGAIN

"No. It just needed some minor adjustments. I told the mechanic if he couldn't get it to running better, I would turn it back."

"But I will need it for school, Dad."

"Ah, Gilla, that old car wasn't worth much anyway. I'll get you a humdinger of a vehicle when I get my factory revved up."

"You got Mister B's property?"

"Not yet. That's the aggravation of it!" he pounded his fist on the table. "There is a stupid law that says I must wait six months to take possession. Six months!"

"But why?"

"Dumb reasons. In case someone shows up with a legal claim on it. They have to run newspaper notices and comb the countryside for creditors that might hold a lien on the old chicken coop. It is foolish and unnecessary. Everybody knows that all the old man's family died years ago. Who would have a scrap of paper to prove ownership? Nobody!"

"Six months isn't very long."

"Next February! Why, I could have my plant in full swing by then!" He flung out his hand as though he would sweep the long wait aside. "What if the war is over by then? What if there is no need for ammunition by February?"

"That would be wonderful! Ju—, the soldiers would all get to come home."

"That would be tragic."

"At least you still have a job, Dad."

"I have no job. I quit work after the old man died so I could begin the big project."

A tiny nucleus of fear lodged at the back of Gilla's

mind. "Then how shall you finance my schooling?"

"There are ways." He made a clucking sound. "With your help we can manage it."

"I'll be glad to help, Dad, for I must get my education. A—a lot depends upon it."

"Yes, I will need a CPA in my business."

"And I will need the income to make my own way in life."

"A loan won't be hard to get. Mr. Fitzwaren, the bank president, knows that I will soon strike it rich. I am a good customer, the kind financiers like. It is most important that we, you and I, establish a good rapport, a close relationship with Mr. Fitzwaren and his family."

"I shall be glad to meet with Mrs. Fitzwaren." Gilla wondered later why she didn't see the ax falling. "And friendship with the banker shouldn't be hard for you, Dad."

"No. People are merely so many cats who, with the right ear rubbing, can be made to purr. That is what made me think up the nice little coming-home surprise I have for you."

No! Not the date with Devon Fitzwaren! Gilla appealed to God to expel the panic that tore at her stomach. Just yesterday she had found peace and happiness, and today the enemy of her soul was trying to rob her of the victory she had gained. It was her first battle, and she must win! She felt weak and tremulous all over. Her voice stiffened. "What surprise, Dad?"

He leaned close and lowered his voice. "Oh, it is the most clever conspiracy. I have arranged a date for you and Mr. Fitzwaren's son. I furnished tickets for the two of you to go to a dance at the country club next weekend.

You will sweep the young Fitzwaren off his feet. I've never seen a swain that didn't eat out of your hand on the first date."

"But, Dad—"

"Remember that a nice loan for me and a college education for you rest on your performance at this dance. So dance, honey, dance!" His rough laugh filled the room.

"Dad, I'm trying to tell you—"

"Every single girl in town would give her best lipstick for your chance! Won't you be the envy? You saw what a dasher the guy was when he brought you home. Your ride, my dear, was preplanned, too. You have a crafty old dad! Now, how do you like my little surprise?"

"I can't go."

"Of course, you can go. If it is the matter of a ball gown, charge it at Miss Amelia's."

"That's not it—"

"I gave fifty dollars each for the tickets, and, of course, you will go and do us up proud. Whatever the problem, we will take care of it. Now have sweet dreams. We will discuss it at length tomorrow. My head is pounding."

Gilla heard her father's footsteps fade across the hall and up the stairs.

Tomorrow.

EIGHTEEN

Dismissed

Had Gil been more alert that Monday evening, he probably would have sensed the change in his daughter, but his perception was dulled by the alcohol he had imbibed. However, on Tuesday morning after a long siege of sleep, his mind proved keener.

For half the night, Gilla had prayed for grace, knowing she would need all the spiritual fortitude she could muster when daylight forced upon her the new and dreaded day. Whatever the results, she would not give up her commitment to God.

At breakfast, Gil was ready to resume the talk he had abandoned the night before. "Now, Gilla, after we eat, I will take you to Miss Amelia's to buy an evening gown. I want you to choose something chic and modern, a style that a young man might consider provocative. Something off the shoulder. Your entrance at the country club must be the focal point of a hundred eyes, making heads turn and bringing envious whispers. You are a Carmichael, daughter of an important man. You have been in enough beauty pageants to know your way around."

Gilla heard, but her mind was indifferent to his prattle. Her thoughts had crept back to Amarillo, back to the living room of her mother's stucco cottage where her heart had taken wings and the Holy Spirit had filled her. A smile pulled at her lips.

Gil misread the smile. "Ah, that mystic, dreamy look in your eyes! It gets them every time. You are a heart stealer, Gilla. How about a fitted dress in midnight black with diamond buttons?"

"What did you say?"

"Where is your mind, Gilla?"

"I was thinking of what I will do when I graduate from college, Dad."

"You will marry the banker's son and work for me!" he supplied. "What has that to do with the topic at hand?"

"Devon Fitzwaren will not want me, nor I him. Our values are poles apart."

"What are you talking about, Gilla? Your values are synonymous. The Fitzwarens go to our church! We were thrilled that they conscripted a pew, and it is right beside our own, quite convenient for you and the young man to make eyes. Mr. Fitzwaren will be a great financial boon to us. He'll be put on the board at the next meeting, to be sure."

The time had come for Gilla to speak; there was no need to evade the issue any longer. "Dad, I am not going to the dance. I would not be comfortable there—"

"I will buy whatever it takes to make you comfortable."

"It isn't a matter of clothes; it is a matter of conscience. I met God while I was gone, and He is my Master. I now walk a different road—"

Gil leaped to his feet and pushed his face toward her. "You will not be a religious crackpot, Gilla Carmichael! I sent you away to make you forget the holy-holy stuff. You

DISMISSED

will accept the date I have arranged for you, and you will make your old man proud of you. I am trying to help you, and you are making it hard for me!"

"I'm sorry, Dad, but I have made up my mind." Calmness washed over her, and she talked on. "Since my personal Pentecost, I have been at peace inside. I find that I cannot go back to your church. I know that you do not understand, and I wish you did. Nonetheless, I have been born again, and the things that once interested me no longer do."

"But a college education does?"

"Y—yes."

"You will go to the dance with Devon Fitzwaren or forfeit your education."

It was a blow. A hard one. She was depending on the education to support her crippled mother. But she could not compromise her convictions. "Very well," she said. "Then I will forfeit my education."

Gil's visage turned cold, stony. "I will not have you make a laughingstock of me in this town!" he roared. "If you cannot obey me, I will disown you. I will turn you out! Without money. Without a home. Then what do you think you will do?"

"I don't know, but I am sure that God will take care of me." Her spirit was wounded, her voice a thin thread of sound. She had expected that there would be a vehement argument, but she didn't expect this.

She was seeing an aspect of her father that made her recoil. When he discovered that she could not be molded, that she stood firm in her tracks, he had viciously turned against her. Is this what her mother had faced?

"Go to your room, Gilla," her father spat. "Go to think

on your rashness and on your future. Then come back down in an hour when you understand your foolishness and have regained your senses. When you come back, I want to see a change of attitude. Then we will go to town." His thick brows came together, and his eyes burned with anger, gray and steady.

"There is no reason for me to spend an hour needlessly," she said. "I shall not change my mind. My faith stands unmoved. I am sorry to be a disappointment to you, but death itself cannot separate me from my relationship with God. Please, try to understand, Dad."

Gil was in no mood to be cajoled. A demon of temper had seized him. He raved at her. "You are just like your mother! Just as pious and just as bent on destroying me! She left, and you can leave, too!"

"But, Dad, I don't want to leave. I want—"

"Leave! I am giving you one hour to be out of my house! You are no longer welcome here! You are no longer my daughter. You are Cassandra Carmichael's daughter!" He was bellowing now. Like the eruption of a volcano, his words gushed from a deep, pent-up force.

Gilla fled to her room. She stood at the window, unable to shut her mind against her father's tirade. Did he mean it? Surely he would reconsider, would stand and would block her exit, offering his apologies when she took her bags downstairs to obey his impulsive command.

But what if he did not recant? Where would she go? Shoulders squared, she began packing the merest of necessities. How much could she carry? How long would she be gone before her father changed his mind and came looking for her? In its usual vein, his anger was like the sputtering of a damp firecracker, soon fizzled.

DISMISSED

Hairbrush. Nightgown. Underwear. Shoes. Hose. She would have to find a job. Hat. Gloves. Where would a seventeen-year-old find employment? Purse. Jacket. Fall was coming; it might get cold. Surely her father wouldn't let her stay out until winter. Scarf. Handkerchiefs. Fright was beginning to blend itself with the uncertainty in her mind. She hadn't enough money for a room tonight. A parasol. Her Bible . . .

She slipped on a skirt under her dress to save space in the suitcase. Could she take everything she would need? The minutes ticked away, dwindling the hour to seconds. Still she lingered. What else . . . ? She wanted to cry but couldn't.

"It is time for you to go, Gilla," her father called from the other side of her door, his voice holding no leniency. "And I am asking that you do not return until you have given up your stubbornness about religion, until you can sit on the pew I am paying for. For if you do return except under these conditions, I will turn you away."

Joseph. Joseph was sold, sent into exile by his own family. At seventeen.

Gil sat stoically in his chair, reading his newspaper as she left. "Good-bye, Dad," she called softly. She was sure he heard her, but he gave no indication of it.

She would have to find immediate employment to support herself, but she wasn't ready for that challenge today. Her mind was too befuddled. She needed a haven where she could think, plan, and pray. A place where she could be alone with her feelings. Where would she find a sanctuary for her bruised heart?

Her cases were heavy and bulky. She found it necessary to sit them down often to rest her arms. Could she

MISTER B'S LAND

make it to the river? It had seemed a short way when she drove her car to Mister B's property, but it would be a great distance by foot. The day was before her, however, and she could think of nowhere else to go.

Ere many blocks were accomplished, an automobile skidded to a stop beside her. "Well, if it isn't Gilla Carmichael, the beauty queen," hurrahed Devon Fitzwaren, "and looking more like a traveling missionary. Can I give you a lift home?"

Gilla offered a smile that cost her a great sacrifice. "Thank you, sir, but I am going for a walk."

"You seem to be taking your whole wardrobe with you," he ribbed. "Are you sure you are not eloping?"

"It has never crossed my mind." She tried hard to be pleasant.

He spun away, leaving black tire marks on the pavement, and Gilla trudged on. If she could just make it beyond the city limits, she would be away from the public's curious stares. She forged on, and once out of town, she slowed down, took more rest stops.

Fortunately, she went along the back of Mr. Brumley's land and not down the dirt road. For had she traveled the road, she would have seen the "NO TRESPASSING" signs posted boldly along the fence.

On the bank of the river, she sat down, exhausted. She was glad the land did not belong to her father yet; he would not want her here. But Mister B would be glad his land could be an asylum for her.

Many and tormenting were Gilla's thoughts as she sat on the spot where she caught her first fish. That seemed an eternity ago. Now the hopes of a college education had deserted her. She would not be able to care for her moth-

DISMISSED

er. The thoughts of writing to tell Cassandra Carmichael that her plans had turned to ashes gave Gilla a sinking feeling in the pit of her stomach. Her mother, who had suffered so much already, would be bitterly disappointed. There would be no trips to Amarillo, no rented post office box for communication, and no way to provide for their future together. Anyway, she hadn't pencil, paper, or stamps to relay the sad news. When her mother didn't hear from her, she would think— Oh, that projection was too painful!

Gilla had been up a substantial part of the night before, and her body was tired. She lay her head on her suitcase and fell asleep. While she slept, the sun dipped into the river, and all the colors faded from the sky, leaving it smoky with dusk.

The sound of locusts awoke her, and she looked about frantically. She hadn't time to get back to town before dark. And if she did go back, where would she spend the night? Hunger gnawed at her middle.

Mr. Brumley, bless his departed soul, surely would welcome her to sleep in his hut tonight. Tomorrow she would be able to think more clearly.

She made her way to the old fellow's shack, went inside, and made herself comfortable on the lumpy mattress with its rusty iron bedstead.

She knew nothing more until morning.

NINETEEN

TOUGH LOVE

Gil ran his fingers through his tousled hair and strode to the kitchen, his mind seething. The frown on his face grew deeper, and he forced his jaw forward as he habitually did in moments of specific displeasure.

Gilla must be taught a much-needed lesson. She had been mollycoddled, spoiled to having her way. It was time for tough love. *Tough love.* Perverse excitement joined his stubborn resolution, fusing into a nameless form of mastery. When Gilla got hungry enough, she would come crawling back, ready to see things his way. When she returned, he might do a bit of compromising himself. But not on church attendance.

She had walked east from Maple, and he suspected she had gone to Peggy Gossimer's. Peggy was Gilla's best friend, and that was the direction in which Peggy lived. Being a pal, Peggy would welcome Gilla or even hide her. This realization caused Gil but slight angst. The arrangement wouldn't last. Peggy planned marriage right away, and her apartment would be too small to house three people. Then Gilla would be forced back home.

She might take herself to the city park for a few hours, but she would soon tire of sitting on hard park benches. Yes, she would be purged from her self-will soon. Then she would be putty in his hands again. Docile. Malleable.

It was just as well that the finance company picked up her car. Heaven only knew where she would have gone if she had a car! As far as her gasoline would have taken her, no doubt.

Gil had always felt that Gilla should justify and repay him with her own future and brilliantly for the time and effort he had spent on her. He had never reflected upon any other outcome but that of his own choosing for her. But suppose she turned out like her mother?

He had tried to steer his daughter from any knowledge of or identity with her mother. Cassandra had enjoyed music. The day she left, Gil sold her piano so Gilla would not be tempted to love the instrument also. Cassandra had played such nerve-wracking tunes, mostly religious.

Since Cassandra had been influenced by a friend, Gil encouraged Gilla's friendship with the upper class. That seemed safe territory. Then she had dragged up that Judo fellow, a pigeon in the aviary. Gil congratulated himself that he had stifled the romance, pleased that the young nonconformist was now in the army. It would suit Gil if the boy never returned. It took a few white lies, but Gil had circumvented Gilla's mail, and she would never know about the letters. Someday she would thank him for his sagacity.

Surely Gilla would be back by Saturday night in time for the dance. But on the remote chance that she wouldn't, Gil felt his responsibility to apprise the banker's son. He needed to stay in the good graces of the Fitzwarens. The boy would understand, would be patient with the moods of a teenage girl trying to find herself. She would be worth his wait.

Gil made his way to town and found Devon Fitzwaren loitering outside the bank, charming a flock of giggling females. "Oh, hello, Mr. Carmichael," he called. "It is good to see you."

"May I speak with you, please?"

"Why, certainly."

"It is about Saturday night—"

"Your daughter has already told me that she cannot go. She is making preparations for college, she said, and needs to do the laundry. I thought that you would not wish the expensive ticket wasted, so I took the liberty to invite another young lady to fill her place."

"I predict that Gilla will change her mind," Gil said. "She went to visit a friend, but I expect her back soon."

"Yes, I saw her leaving with her luggage, and I offered her a lift. She said she preferred to walk."

"Did she seem happy?"

"She was in a great mood. All smiles. I thought she might be eloping; she was toting a lot of baggage for a short stay!"

"There is always the slight possibility that she will not get back in time for the dance. Gilla—ah—isn't herself right now. The usual growing-up syndrome. But she'll get her head on straight."

"Surely. Don't worry about your attractive daughter, Mr. Carmichael. All of us in the modern generation have to try our wings. Let her have her little fantasy flight—"

"And crash. And get her wings sheared off."

"Exactly. That is her privilege. We in 1941 just rebel in different ways than you did back in 1921."

Gil whistled around the corner, feeling cheered. That young Fitzwaren was a perceptive chap; he'd make a good match for Gilla. Preoccupied, Gil almost ran headlong into Peggy Gossimer. "Oh, Mr. Carmichael!" She sidestepped. "I very nearly tripped you!"

"My fault," he laughed. "How are you, Miss Gossimer?"

"I couldn't be better, sir. And how is Gilla enjoying her vacation? I haven't heard a word from her! When is she coming home? I need to talk with her about the wedding. I do want her for a bridesmaid, remember. I am on my way to pick up the material for her dress now."

"Gilla isn't home."

"As soon as she gets in, will you have her contact me, please, Mr. Carmichael?"

"I expect her in soon, and I will give her your message."

"Thank you."

So Gilla wasn't at Peggy's. What other friends did she have? Or she might have kept out enough money from her trip to rent a room. That was a probability. But her money wouldn't last long. She had never managed money, and the paying of bills would eat up what little she had in no time. An indulged child had no concept of the high cost of living.

Then a new notion struck Gil. It hit so forcefully that he stopped in the middle of the sidewalk to assimilate it with all its ramifications. Gilla would try to get a job to support herself just to show him that she could! He would have to nip that in the bud, head it off. If she found a way to get food and shelter, she might prolong her dereliction. She must be whipped into line with hunger and homelessness and need.

There were few places in town that would hire minors.

TOUGH LOVE

The steam laundry was one. They paid twenty-five cents an hour for a ten-hour day. Only the most desperate of humanity worked there, and it would humiliate him to no end if she should show up at such a place. She wouldn't, because he would see that she didn't!

To the laundry Gil rushed and asked to speak to the manager.

"How may I help you, sir?" asked the greasy-haired boss.

"I have a daughter whom I am trying to discipline," he explained.

"And you want me to hire her?"

"No, I dare you to hire her! She is trying to bypass my rules, and it is possible that she will look for work here. She is not of legal age and is still my dependent. If you hire her, you will be undermining my parental strategy, and I will press charges against your establishment for interference."

"Of course, sir, I understand your position and agree with what you are trying to do," the manager nodded. "If there were more disciplinarians such as yourself, there would be less delinquency. If she comes, we will not give her a job. What is her name?"

"Gilla Carmichael."

He wrote it down and taped it to the cash register.

Next Gil went to the cafeterias and gave the same warning. They sometimes hired underage dishwashers. He went to the sewing factory, the bakery, and the secondhand store. They all agreed to refuse Gilla employment should she ask it of them.

Finally, Gil hurried to the newspaper office and ran a notice in the classified section stating that he did not wish his daughter to be hired by anyone until she finished college.

Satisfied that he had blocked every avenue Gilla might pursue to support herself, he went back to Maple Street, smiling smugly.

She would be home in a matter of hours.

TWENTY

Miss Joseph

It was a damp daybreak. A cloudy haze hung over the river, shrouding it with whiteness. Gilla sat on the dew-laden bank, trying to catch a fish for her breakfast. The fish weren't cooperating this morning.

Then as the sun rose, the fog crept away, and the sky gleamed through in frayed patches of blue. All that remained were diaphanous puffs of vapor on the mirrored surface of the water, which soon ebbed to nothing.

This was a splendid place. Gilla wished she might stay here forever, separated from the world, not having to worry about winter or food or a way to make a living for herself. However, as soon as she caught her meal and gained enough strength for the walk into town, she must search for a job. Yesterday she'd had no luck.

She would take any job as long as it was honest work. Washing dishes, sweeping floors, tending children, cooking . . . Wrapped in her contemplation, she did not hear the approaching voices until they were very near her. She crept behind a bush and tried to squeeze herself into invisibility, hoping feverishly that the leaves would conceal her. Two men in wide-brimmed panamas passed so near that she held her breath.

"What do you think this plot of land will bring?" asked one.

MISTER B'S LAND

"At least thirty dollars an acre."

"That's much too high, Bill. That's scaring five thousand dollars!"

"This is top-dollar land, and it's on the river. It is also near town. Several prosperous businessmen have their eyes fastened on it. Especially Mr. Carmichael."

"The former tax assessor?"

"Yes. And the first thing he wants to do is set fire to the old cabin and clear the land of trees. He plans to turn it into a manufacturing compound. Claims he'll make a million."

"When does it come up for public auction?"

"The law requires a six-month wait in case someone shows up with a will."

"And there's no chance of that, I suppose?"

"No chance. The old man was ninety-three, and he left no one alive to pick up the spoil."

The men moved on, and their voices died away. Gilla stayed sequestered for another hour to make sure they were gone. Then she resumed her fishing but still caught nothing. Not wanting to waste more precious time, she trudged back to the cabin and boiled some cornmeal in water to make a weak mush. She hated to use so much of the scarce commodity, but she had to have some food.

Yesterday she had worn her best dress to make her job applications and had been turned down at every establishment she tried. Perhaps she was overdressed for common employment. Today she would wear a simple skirt and blouse, which would give her a hearty look. Today she would find a job.

All day, she plodded from company to company without getting even a proper interview. She had no idea that

MISS JOSEPH

jobs were so difficult to find. Last of all, she went to the laundry. "I am Gilla Carmichael, and I am looking for—"

The proprietor began shaking his head and made a wall with his hands. "No work for you, missy. I have your name right here in black and white. It says, 'Do not hire Gilla Carmichael.'"

"Why do you have my name, and why should I not be hired?"

"Your father came in earlier this week and told us not to employ you. You are not of age, and your father's word is law. What you had best do is hie yourself back home where you belong and come under subjection to your father. We have all been duly warned about you, and none of us would dare put you to work for a single hour. We could be sued. We don't interfere between parents and their children."

Gilla's mind reeled with disbelief. Her father had sabotaged her chances of supporting herself! How dare he! As if turning her out was not hurtful enough, he was determined that she would suffer starvation.

And she could not return home, he had specified, unless she was willing to give up her relationship with God. Well, she would rather die, and it looked like that might be her fate.

As she passed Abe's Car Lot on her way out of town, she saw her own roadster parked there with a "For Sale" sign in the window. She fought an unexpected stab of bitterness.

Joseph didn't let bitterness destroy him.

With great effort, Gilla dug out the root of gall that tried to plant itself in her soul. She would pray for her father instead of hating him.

But what would she do without money? Without food? She should have stayed in Amarillo! Had she known that she would be turned out, would be denied her education, she would have remained with her mother. Surely she could have found some small job there.

Was Joseph ever this frightened?

Well, at least Mister B had left a great pile of wood for the pot-bellied stove, some candles, and matches. There was little food, but the fish might decide to bite before dark.

By the time Gilla reached the perimeter of the property, the hard light of day had softened. She sniffed. Rain. She had forgotten to bring her umbrella. Accelerating her pace, she cast uneasy glances upward. At both ends of the horizon, two sliding doors of gray clouds were closing off the sunshine.

She wanted to cry. *Did Joseph ever cry?*

Splatters of rain kicked up dust at her feet as she reached the shack's front door. From the looks of things, there would be no more fishing today. Supper would be mush again, using the last of the meal left in the old crock canister.

The sky grew darker. Then the rain came, rods of water. Lightning rippled in violent flashes. Mere seconds split the brightest flashes from the cracking of the thunder. Bang! Crash! Boom! She covered her ears.

But the storm didn't live long. It moved out, leaving the roof dripping water into the small room.

That evening, Gilla crawled beneath Mr. Brumley's tattered quilt and lay for a long time before drifting into an unsettled sleep. Faceless fears rose up around her, and she awoke at every sound. "Lord," she asked, "what do You want me to do?"

MISS JOSEPH

She welcomed daylight. Arising as soon as it was light enough to see, she dipped her bath water from the rain barrel outside. Then adding a kettle of scalding water in Mister B's old tin tub, she bathed and washed her hair, feeling much refreshed.

When she had dressed, she reached for the old man's Bible instead of her own. It opened to the Gospel according to Luke, chapter nine. She began to read what he had marked. *For whosoever will save his life, shall lose it: but whosoever will lose his life for my sake, the same shall save it. For what is a man advantaged, if he gain the whole world, and lose himself, or be cast away?*

Gilla closed the Bible and, still pondering the verses, stepped to the outhouse. On the way back, her eyes fell on a bed of brown straw that she had not noticed before. The rain had flattened the weeds around it, deepening its color, making it conspicuous. Why this one dead patch of grass?

She moved closer to have a look and discovered that the door to a cellar lay beneath the camouflage. The door creaked open as she pulled at the metal ring, exposing a deep, dark hole in the ground. She could see nothing but blackness.

Her flashlight! It was packed away in the bottom of her suitcase. She ran for it and descended dirt steps into the bowels of the earth. Here it was dry and musty.

Flashing her beam about, she found a vast supply of food stacked against the earthen walls. A quick inventory showed a tall milk can of meal and an identical one of flour. A tow sack filled with dried corn. Wild honey. Dried fruit. Pinto beans. Rice. A jug of molasses. Salt. A large

MISTER B'S LAND

crock of lard. Lye soap. Bins of potatoes and onions. A large box of Post Toasties. Candles and matches in abundance. And an assortment of tins marked "Corned Beef," "Chili," and "Canned Milk."

There were garden seeds of all kinds. She could plant a garden if she were here next spring. Of course, she wouldn't be. After February, her father would own the land, and her home would be razed. According to the strangers she heard talking, he planned to burn it.

But she would not think of next spring. She would be grateful for these provisions. Here in this underground vault were staples enough to last all winter. With the fresh fish she could catch, she would have no worries of going hungry. Evidently, this was God's storehouse!

Joseph had plenty of food in the time of famine. . . .

Miss Joseph. That's what the old man had called her. Memory put a smile on Gilla's face. If he could see her now!

TWENTY-ONE

THE DOCTOR'S REPORT

Cassandra Carmichael was losing the use of her arms. A frightening numbness had settled in them. "Thomas," she said, "I think that I shall be paralyzed and completely useless except to boss you around."

"We will get you to Dr. Varner to see what he says," suggested her brother, "for I certainly don't want to be bossed."

"Doctor's appointments are costly."

"I will take a second job."

"Oh, no, Thomas—"

"Now, don't start bossing yet. I will have my way as long as I can," he teased.

They learned that Cassandra's doctor had closed his office and had left town. "I can't bear the thoughts of breaking in another doctor," she fretted. "Dr. Varner knew all about me. A new one will have to start over with questions and tests."

"We will do what we must, Dawn," insisted Thomas. "I will drive down to the hospital and request a physician who has studied bones."

"Oh, Thomas! You must not get a specialist. The cost will be prohibitive."

"No bossing, Dawn."

MISTER B'S LAND

Thomas found the name of a doctor just beginning his practice in Amarillo and took Cassandra to him. His name was Wade.

Dr. Wade was a likable chap albeit too young to trust with one's health, Cassandra felt. But Thomas had said he had excellent recommendations, so she tried to ignore his apple-fresh cheeks and boyish hands. He couldn't be over thirty years of age!

Cassandra answered his questions, rather perturbed that his inquisitiveness reached so far into her past. He particularly probed into her previous diagnosis and medication. It was almost as if he were doubting the credentials of her former doctors, who were much older than he.

He said she needed a thorough examination, an opinion with which she disagreed. When he moved her extremities very gently, he asked if there was any suffering. Was there pain in the joints? In the bones? In the muscles? Cassandra assured him that there was none.

He looked puzzled. Could she move her legs? he asked. Her toes? Bend her knees? Yes, she said. She had no problems doing all those things. He pursed his lips, and his rust-colored brows bumped the rims of his thick glasses.

He put more pressure on her limbs. "Does that hurt?"

"No, sir."

"And how long have you been in a wheelchair?"

"For ten years."

"Why?"

"Because my doctor said that the bones in my legs would break if I should put my body's weight on them. They are brittle. The arthritis is a rare form, a degenerative kind."

THE DOCTOR'S REPORT

"Was there pain when he diagnosed your case?"

"Oh, yes. There was terrible pain. But with medication, the pain went away."

"Did the doctor who diagnosed your arthritis x-ray your bones?"

"No, sir."

"We need x-rays."

"But, sir, we haven't insurance."

"Mr. McLellan said that I should proceed with whatever testing is necessary, and x-rays are necessary."

With the testing ended, Dr. Wade set up a return appointment for Cassandra. He would need time to study the x-rays, he said.

"See, Thomas, he will keep us coming back," Cassandra worried on the way home. "It is the way of this new generation of medical men. You will never be able to pay the bill. I don't want to leave you with a big debt when I go to live with my daughter."

"Dawn, I've warned you about getting your hopes fixed on Gilla. You didn't rear her, and it is likely that she has already returned to her father's society. It has been a month since she left, and you have not heard a word from her. I say no news is not good news in this case. I am planning to care for you for the rest of your life. Bossing or no bossing."

"Gilla had integrity, Thomas. I don't know why I haven't heard from her, but she will not turn her back on God or the experience she received here."

"Being with you would make a child want to have integrity, my brave sister. But teenagers are impressionable. She had good intentions, yes. However, the ability to follow through on those intentions is another story.

Remember, she is yet under the jurisdiction of her father."
Thomas was right, of course. Cassandra didn't like to be reminded that she had made grand plans of fragile material, fabric that might rip and shred, exposing her battered heart. But it was true. If Gilla was going to write, surely she would have done so already. Anyway, why should a young and healthy girl be saddled with a helpless mother, emotionally or otherwise?

All that week, Cassandra fought the demons of discouragement, and when the time came for her to return to the doctor, she refused to go. "He can tell you what he found with his high-powered machinery," she told Thomas. "I don't want to go back."

Thomas took off his job at the stockyards to keep the appointment.

"Why didn't your sister come?" asked the doctor.

"Of late, she doesn't like to get out of the house," was his oblique reply. "She has always tried to keep up her morale, but with this latest development, I'm afraid she is losing the battle."

"I had hoped that I might talk with her in person, for I have made a shocking discovery. Her bones are in perfect condition, as good as mine or yours. She has no arthritis; she has never had arthritis. Somewhere along the line, she was misdiagnosed. The medication she has been taking is creating the problem, that is, the weakness and numbness. It is too strong for her heart. When the medicine is discontinued, she will be quite normal."

"Excuse me, sir, but are you saying that she can walk?"

"Not today."

"But someday?"

THE DOCTOR'S REPORT

"Indeed. Her muscles are weak from lack of use. If she tried to stand, she would fall. She needs therapy, but it is something she can do on her own. I will send her a list of strength-building exercises to practice. She should be running a marathon in a few months."

Thomas sat in silence. "You are sure of this, sir?"

"Ninety-nine percent certain."

Thomas didn't return to work. He headed for home so fast that a policeman stopped him.

"Where is the fire, mister?" the officer asked.

"Inside of me!" grinned Thomas. "The doctor just told me that my sister, who hasn't walked in ten years, is going to walk. I'm on my way to tell her so."

"Then go, sir," the lawman said, "but a little more slowly, please."

Not expecting Thomas until suppertime, Cassandra had given vent to a bout of tears. Despair lurked nearby. Thomas must not know; he must not suspect that she no longer wished to live. She would do her weeping while he was gone so he wouldn't think her unthankful for all the sacrifices he had made for her. To what avail were those sacrifices? She would soon be a total invalid.

Thomas burst through the door, calling her name, "Cassandra Dawn."

She turned her head so he could not see her tear-blotched face.

"Look at me."

She turned puffy eyes toward him.

"The doctor said—"

"I don't care what he said, Thomas. I won't go back. I won't even take my medication anymore. I'm sorry, Thomas, but I don't want to live like this—"

"That is exactly what the doctor said."

"That I won't live?"

"That you won't live like that! That you should discontinue your medication because it isn't doing you any good. That you will likely not come to see him again." He laughed. "You are following orders well."

"Forgive me, Thomas, but I—"

"Now, listen to me, sis. There is nothing wrong with you. Do you hear me? There is nothing wrong with your legs! Or your arms! You don't have arthritis. Your bones are in perfect order. With exercise and the building of your lazy muscles, you can jump rope. The medicine is causing your disability. Throw it away. Today." He pitched Dr. Wade's instructions into her lap. "There. You are whole. You are not a cripple. Start working hard, and you will be walking in a matter of months."

"Don't tease, Thomas."

"I am not joking. It looks as though you won't get to boss me around after all."

TWENTY-TWO

WAR!

November flamed with colors of an aging year—scarlets, saffrons, and jades—while the wayside ferns formed a bright filigree of golds and rusts. Here the season seemed to stall before making its final change to winter.

Mister B had nailed a calendar to the wall, a feed-store edition with the picture of a red barn on it, and Gilla marked off the days as they passed. Time slipped by subtly, each day bringing her closer to vagrancy.

Her bright dreams for the future were buried: a college education, a good job, providing a home for her crippled mother. Judo, though, she could not banish from her heart. Sometimes his presence seemed so close that she could imagine him beside her, telling her to take courage, holding her hand. She prayed for him every night.

Since there was little to distract her, she began a study of the Bible from front to back, reading slowly. The perusal sponged up many vacuous hours. When she needed to rest her eyes, she went outside and gathered nuts and winter grapes. She kept her clothes washed and her small area clean, falling into a comfortable ritual.

Now and then she walked to the gasoline station that sat on the hem of the town. She made a practice of reading the headlines of the newspaper in the rack. Most of

the stories concerned the war that was raging in Europe.
Then the calendar had only one leaf: December. Winter was late arriving, but that was not unusual for central Texas. The nights were cold, but the days were pleasant enough. Gilla was prepared for the frigid season with the supplies brought from the cellar to the house.

Another week passed, and on the seventh day of the month, a west wind brought the clear sound of the fire whistle in town. Other sirens joined in the mighty wail. It sounded as if the whole of the city must be on fire. Gilla looked toward town but could see no smoke. The whistle sounded for a very long while.

The next morning, Gilla donned Mister B's old mackintosh and went to see what had been destroyed. When she passed the newspaper stand at the station, she stopped in her tracks. Pearl Harbor had been bombed! The United States had declared war on Japan! Over two thousand soldiers were killed, their names yet to be released. The sirens had cried for the whole city.

She stumbled back to her hideout, appalled by the news. The whole world was going out of control. *Judo, where are you?* What could she do to help her shaken country?

Time went by fits and starts. Hours and minutes staggered strangely out of focus. A bitter cold moved in as if to present an analogy of the cold war that mushroomed. Gilla wished desperately that she had a radio.

When she could stand the suspense no longer, she wrapped up as good as she was able and started out to see what information she could garner. The cold cut through her hose and into her flimsy shoes, biting at her feet. Her calves felt as if they had been slit by a knife in

WAR!

need of sharpening. She tried to breathe through the scarf about her mouth, but no breath was ever deep enough. Yet she had to make it to town!

The newspaper rack at the station was empty. Area citizens gobbled up every trace of news they could find.

In hopes that someone might have a battery-operated radio that she could get near enough to hear, she walked on to the city park. The chilly day daunted park visitors, but an elderly gentleman sat on a wooden bench digesting the paper, his collar pulled up around his ears. Gilla inched toward him, hoping to read over his shoulder, but was disappointed that he kept moving the publication, turning pages.

At last, he folded it. "Pardon me, sir," she spoke up. "If you are finished with the newspaper, may I sit here and read it? I will give it back."

He flapped his gloved hand. "I'm through with it, missy. You may have it. But I can't imagine anyone with eyes as pretty as yours reading about something this ugly." He handed the paper to her.

Her toes were numb with cold. She could feel the stiff leather of her shoes chafing against her heels and feared it would rub blisters. But in spite of the discomfort, she ran all the way to the cabin. It looked like it might start snowing any minute.

The first page of the paper gave the rundown of events leading to the war. Determined to stay neutral, President Roosevelt had met Winston Churchill on the high seas, and they had formulated the Atlantic Charter, a general statement of democratic aim. It helped nothing. Five United States battleships were sunk on a peaceful Hawaiian island, and 140 airplanes destroyed. The paper

MISTER B'S LAND

printed small maps so American readers could follow the Japanese movement. The last civilian autos were rolling off the assembly line in Detroit, and as German submarines came near the coast of Georgia, the citizens' army—those too young, too old, or too unfit for the draft—set about preparing coastal defenses for an anticipated German invasion. Draft notices were appearing in many mailboxes, and the nation's fittest were enlisting by droves.

On the second page, she found it. There was Judo's picture with an accompanying article: *Son of local businessman among casualties.* Jude O. Franklin, along with his whole regiment, lost his life when his ship was torpedoed by a submarine in the South Pacific, the report stated. A memorial service would be held for him in Wilson's Funeral Parlor on Wednesday.

Gilla gripped the iron headboard dizzily. Her stomach heaved as the hurt submerged. How long she sat there waiting for hope to draw its final, rattling breath, she did not know. Time without hope was meaningless. She must be hungry after the long walk to town, but she couldn't feel it.

Judo. Her Judo. She couldn't go on. She could not even think. All she could do was bawl like a baby until the moaning subsided to jerky sobs. The sobs shook her to sleep, and in a glorious dream she saw the angels lift Judo into their arms and bear him tenderly away to a mother who waited.

She clipped Judo's picture from the paper and placed it in her Bible. She would go to his funeral. Wednesday. Two days hence.

However, when she awoke on Wednesday, a heavy

WAR!

snow covered the ground, a deep drift blocking the door. She would not be able to get to town to pay her last respects to her only friend. She would not be among the mourners to tell Judo good-bye.

The shack cracked and snapped as the cold tightened its grip.

TWENTY-THREE

Two Calls

Gil Carmichael was an opportunist. He put extensive study into the tenor of the war. When, a few days after the Pearl Harbor attack, Germany and Italy declared war on the United States, he knew the time to make his move had come.

The Allies were suffering disastrous defeats in the Pacific. An entire Allied fleet went down in the Java Sea. In drips and drops came news of those who had been rescued and those who had been left behind, but Gil paid little heed to the number of casualties. All that mattered was that the government was destitute of ample supplies and ammunition, and here was his chance to make a mint.

He sprinted to the lawyer, again taking his briefcase for clout. "Laws can be changed in the event of a national emergency," he said, calculating each word, pretending to know things he didn't. "I need the Brumley place immediately. It has been four months since you advertised in the paper. If you have had no response in four months, it is useless to wait longer. Get the land for me, and when my factory is rolling, I will see that you are generously rewarded."

"You may have a valid point there, Mr. Carmichael. I understand you wanted the land to build a plant that would benefit the government?"

MISTER B'S LAND

"Yes."

"Let me contact the State Capitol to see if we can waive that binder on the land. I agree with you. Enough time has lapsed that we can feel safe in letting it go. Since you are the only one who has plans in the category of service to our government, I think that you will be given priority status. Give me a couple of days, and I will call you."

Gil experienced a delightful tingling of the nerves, half anticipation and half impatience, and with it a shortness of breath as though he had been running. Had he ever felt so excited? That night he allowed himself an extra bottle of wine for celebration. Who cared that the world was in war? War meant opportunities for a clever businessman. He didn't have a son to worry about. He only had a daughter. . . .

He was surprised and a little worried that his daughter hadn't returned. It was taking her longer to come to her senses than he thought it would. Carmichael blood was stubborn blood; a Carmichael didn't give up easy. Although he had no idea where Gilla was, he was convinced that she was keeping close tabs on him. When he struck it rich, she would be there with her hand out for her part of the pot. The object was to make the money so he would be in command, and then everything else would fall in place.

Gil hovered around the phone for the next two days. He had no doubts that his proposal would be accepted or that Mr. Fitzwaren would hand over the money for the purchase of the land. At the snap of his fingers, the construction would start.

When the telephone jangled, he pounced on it like a cat on a mouse. This was his lucky day!

TWO CALLS

"Hello." A professional voice. Businesslike.
"Hello. Gil?"
It was Gilla's voice. She wasn't even giving him the courtesy of the usual "Dad." A bit disconcerting.
"Where are you, Gilla?"
"This isn't Gilla."
"This is Gilla. I would recognize your voice underwater."
"This is Cassandra. I would like to speak with my daughter, please."
Cassandra. After fourteen years of silence. "Gilla is not here."
"Where can I reach her?"
"She has gone out of town for a few days and doesn't wish to be disturbed by a mother she does not even remember."
"When will she return?"
Gil's temper flared. "I am not sure."
"How long has she been gone, Gil?"
"I think that is none of your business!"
"She is my daughter."
"You forfeited your rights to her when you ran away with another man."
"I left with my older brother, Thomas McLellan. I am still with him."
"Your maiden name wasn't McLellan."
"Remember that I was adopted. I took the name of my adoptive parents. My birth name is McLellan."
"I don't care about your family history!"
Cassandra's voice softened. "Are you all right, Gil? You seem to be overwrought about something."
"I couldn't be better, Cassandra. Even as we speak, I

MISTER B'S LAND

am on the verge of becoming the wealthiest man in McLennan County. I thought this call was the one I awaited, the call that will guarantee me a legal claim on some property on which I will build a defense plant. So if you please, Cassandra, don't tie up the line. And don't call back to my house. Ever."

"But I have some good news for Gilla. I wanted to tell her—"

"I don't care what you wanted to tell Gilla. I haven't time to listen and certainly won't relay a message!" Gil slammed down the receiver.

Why her call should unnerve him so, Gil did not pull back the cover to find out. But it did aggravate him. It ruined his whole day. He was still discomposed when Mr. Swaiz called about the land.

"It looks promising, Mr. Carmichael," he said. "There is a mountain of paperwork to be completed, but at least we have the wheels turning."

"How long—?"

"I expect that we can get everything settled for you by the first of the year."

"A pleasant way to start 1942."

"If any of us are here."

"What do you mean by that?"

"We are not holding our own very well in this war."

"When I get my defense plant going, we will show them!"

"And, Mr. Carmichael—?"

"Yes?"

"Someone has been out to the old shack. The rural mail carrier reported seeing smoke coming from the stovepipe. We suspect that a hobo has been camping there."

TWO CALLS

"I argued that the pigsty should be burned to the ground; I will be glad to strike the match."

"Hold on a few days. The sheriff is going tomorrow to roust out the bum. There are 'No Trespassing' signs all over the place. But some of those boxcar bums can't read. The old moocher probably thinks the signs say, 'Welcome, Free Lodging.'" He laughed at his own joke.

"Whoever it is, I don't want them on my land. I have no patience with people who claim to be down on their luck. If they had any ambition or brains, they would be somewhere making money. Like me."

"The sheriff will find out who is on your place and will oust him, Mr. Carmichael. That's what sheriffs are for."

It was the second grain of sand in Gil's craw in less than an hour. It wasn't to celebrate that he sought his bottle this time but to soothe his frayed nerves.

Well, if lightning refused to strike the old shack, Gil Carmichael would. He didn't wish to provide shelter for rats or skunks.

The next day, the date the sheriff promised to check out the report of a vagabond at the old Brumley place, a snowstorm hit with such vengeance that he could not get there. The road was impassable.

Twenty-Four

The Bequest

Trapped in by snowdrifts, Gilla grew restless. She had finished her Bible study and wanted an activity. Her mind craved an outlet.

Once before, she had picked up the strange book written by Paul, Mister B's nephew, and read the last chapter, but it didn't make an ounce of sense. Either it was too deep for her, or the author was batty. But she had started at the wrong end of the book. Perhaps if she began at the first, she could better understand the man's views.

She opened to the flyleaf on which Mister B or someone had penciled a brief message. "God is leading you to page 121. G. W. B." She supposed the G. W. B. stood for G. Wilson Brumley. She followed the curious instructions to the indicated page with the same interest she would render to working a puzzle. Between pages 120 and 121 was a very tattered letter, faded to illegibility. The faint outline of a name at the bottom seemed to be "Rose." And there was a folded note sheet that said, "This is a message for the one whom God has led here."

She unfolded the yellow sheet and read, "To whomever finds this legal document, I, G. Wilson Brumley, being of sound mind, bequeath all my property and assets thereon. Take this last will and testament to the county

MISTER B'S LAND

judge for probation." It was signed and dated April 1, 1910.

The import of the single page soaked into Gilla's brain in small increments. She read it over and over again. "To whomever finds . . ." She had found Mr. Brumley's will!

Scarcely visible at the bottom of page 121 was a notation: "See Page 143." With trembling hands, she turned there and found a sealed envelope of a much later genre. "Open," it instructed. Inside was a crude map directing her to the cash the old man had hidden in a can in the low attic above her.

She stacked her suitcase, clothing, quilts, and a pillow on the bed to reach the loose board. Behind it was the promised can filled with bills. Most were in denominations of tens and twenties, rolled in a piece of brown paper. Gilla counted the money through a curtain of tears. Nearly four thousand dollars! And it was all—hers?

She recalled something Mister B had said about his nephew's book. The book was a failure in the literary world, but Mister B would try to bring it to some value. This then was his reference.

Joseph. No matter where he was put, he always floated to the top.

Miss Joseph. Yes, she understood now why God had impressed Joseph's story on her heart. She had walked in Joseph's shoes. The blessing she had just unearthed wouldn't take Judo's place. It wouldn't erase the injustice inflicted by her father. But she would have a roof over her head, a dwelling that no one could take from her. The picture of a future began to fill the gray blanks into which she had been staring since she left home.

She could even buy a car if she wished! She could fill

THE BEQUEST

the tank with gasoline, and come spring she could drive to Amarillo to see her mother.

When she was eighteen, her father could no longer keep her from getting a job. She would build herself a home on this God-given land and would share it with Cassandra.

The days that followed were days of thanksgiving. She was anxious for the weather to clear so she could take her document into town. Someone—perhaps the judge?—would have to be the guardian of her estate until her eighteenth birthday in April. The time would pass swiftly while she planted a garden and fed the birds and picked bouquets of flowers. . . .

Gilla had on the old man's coat, bringing in firewood, when the sheriff's car stopped in front of the shack. Gilla froze. How did anyone know she was here? She turned her back and continued to pick up sticks.

"Sir," the sheriff's voice was gruff.

Gilla turned to face him. "Uh," the sheriff stammered, "I mean, ma'am. Didn't you see the signs posted on the fence out there?" He jerked his thumb toward the road.

"No, sir. I always come in the back way. By the river."

"Always? How long have you been here?"

"About four months, sir."

"Are you by yourself?"

"Yes, sir."

"A school truant? A runaway?"

"I know I look small in this big coat, sir," smiled Gilla, "but I am older than I look. I am out of high school. I will be eighteen on my next birthday."

"Do you just make yourself at home on other people's property?"

Gilla blushed. "Yes, sir. I mean, no, sir. This is my

MISTER B'S LAND

property now. I have been waiting for the weather to clear so I may go to the judge with my legal papers."

"You are very mistaken, little lady. This land belonged to old G. Wilson Brumley, and he had no relatives. You have come to the wrong place."

Again Gilla smiled. "I know where I am, sir. Truly, I do. But I have Mr. Brumley's will. He willed everything that he had to me."

"I don't mean to be calling you a liar, miss, but I will have to see those papers. I can't just take your word for it."

"Certainly." Gilla went inside and returned with the signed will. The sheriff examined it, took off his hat, and scratched his head. As he put his hat on again, he ejaculated, "Well, blow me down. This paper is legal. Now what will the land buzzards think of this quirk of fate?"

Gilla thought he was addressing her. "I wouldn't know, sir."

"Have you the money to file the affidavit? If you don't, you may have trouble—"

"Yes, sir. Mister B—that is, Mr. Brumley—left me funds for the transfer of deed and—and everything."

"You should get this taken care of at once. Would you like a ride into town?"

"If you don't mind, sir."

"And what is your name, miss?"

"Gilla Carmichael."

"Not—not any kin to Gilbert Carmichael?"

"He is my father."

"Um." He scratched his head again, longer this time. Gilla hoped he didn't have fleas. "That does complicate matters."

THE BEQUEST

"He can't take the land from me, can he, sir? I'm not—quite eighteen."

"Not if the judge is an upright man. We have a new judge, and he doesn't know Gil Carmichael. That will help. Now, I'd say if you took it to a lawyer—"

"No, I will follow Mr. Brumley's instructions."

"A wise old fellow. That was good advice."

He let Gilla out at the courthouse and shook his head in wonderment all the way back to his station.

TWENTY-FIVE

LOST DREAMS

Gilla would be home for Christmas, Gil assured himself, and that time was at hand. Over the years, he had given her elaborate gifts—a fur coat, jewelry, clothing, a cedar chest, vanity sets, gift certificates—and she would conveniently get over her miff in time to see what this year's prize would be. No teenage girl could resist a gift.

What would it be? It would have to be an item he could put on a charge account; his cash reserve was gone. Miss Amelia would likely have something exclusive in her shop. The affluent patronized her boutique.

The ring of the telephone burst in upon Gil's reverie. "Mr. Carmichael?"

"Yes?"

"Attorney Swaiz."

"The paperwork has come through in time for Christmas?"

"I'm afraid, Mr. Carmichael, that I have discouraging news."

"The property won't be available until February," supplied Gil. "Well, February isn't that far removed, Mr. Swaiz. I am not so terribly disillusioned."

"It is worse than that, sir."

"Not a year's wait! It can't happen, Mr. Swaiz. My

credit will not hold out for another year."

"Someone has shown up with a legal will. The property will not come up for sale."

"But surely the owner, whomever he may be, will be agreeable to sell at the price I would be willing to pay. Do you know who he is? Where is he from? How can we contact him?"

"I know very little. The sheriff went out to check on the report of a vagrant in residence on the land and found that the person was within his rights to be there."

"Did anyone see the papers? There could be fraud involved—" He clutched the receiver so hard that his knuckles turned white.

"The sheriff examined the papers. They're bonafide. The new judge is handling the probation of the will."

"Can you find out for me who owns it?"

"As I understand, a minor—and a girl at that—is the sole heir of the land."

"What would a child want with 160 acres of forest and an old shack? The turn of events might actually be to my advantage."

"Could be. Like I say, I haven't much information. You might want to talk with the judge."

"I will do that. Thank you, Mr. Swaiz."

Gil attired himself in his best suit and the hat that made him look taller. He headed for the county courthouse, walking to save gasoline. The small anxiety that rubbed against his mind was no more irritating than a cinder in his shoe. He would buy the land from the heir; it was as simple as that. Money talked. And a child? Her guardian surely would be anxious to rid himself of the responsibility of taxes and upkeep. Owning land cost money, while funds in the bank accumulated money.

In the judge's office, Gil stepped out on the wrong foot without knowing it. "I am Gil Carmichael," he said, and the judge nodded. "You are new here, but I am one of the city's leading citizens."

The judge waited, showing no signs of being impressed.

Gil tried harder. "I worked for the city for some time and have my country's best interests at heart. I want to help. Therefore, I resigned my job to pursue a private enterprise."

"What is your point, Mr. Carmichael?" The judge looked down his long nose at Gil.

All his features are big, thought Gil. *Nose. Ears. Mouth. Chin.* "I've come to talk about some property that you are handling."

"Elaborate further, please."

"I want to buy the old Brumley place, an acreage on the river formerly owned by G. Wilson Brumley, the old fellow who died just before you took office."

"I see. But I must inform you that the property is not for sale."

"In my opinion, sir, there is no property that is inaccessible to a buyer for the right price. I would like to contact the owner of that land to offer a proposal."

"The owner is a minor."

"Then I would like to address his guardian."

"Her guardian. Under the existing circumstances, I have appointed myself her guardian."

"Oh, then it is with you that I must make negotiations."

"The property is not negotiable. It is not for sale at any price."

"What would a child want with a grove of trees and a shanty?"

"A child who has no home is grateful for anything."

"Is this a relative of Mr. Brumley's? A great-niece or something of the sort?"

"No kin. Just someone who loved the old man."

"Local?"

"I am not at liberty to release that information, Mr. Carmichael."

Gil was not accustomed to rebuttal. "And the child had no parents?"

"She has parents. Her mother is disabled, and her father is a lout. I, personally, shall see that she gets the property."

"Will she be able to pay the taxes?"

"She will. Along with the property, the old gentlemen left her a good sum of money. I am keeping it in trust in case her father decides to try to take it from her. I give her an allowance each month such as will amply meet her needs. She is a most lovely child, one of which any parent should be proud. Unfortunately, her father hadn't enough intelligence to appreciate such a daughter. It is my pleasure to serve her to the best of my ability."

Gil did not recognize himself in the portrait done in living color by the judge. His mind clawed for ways to obtain his goal.

"Can you imagine a man who would stoop so low as to turn a sweet child out on the street to starve?" the judge continued.

"Since I have a daughter of my own," Gil said, "I cannot comprehend such a thing."

"How old is your daughter, Mr. Carmichael?"

"She is seventeen."

"Does she live with you?"

"Yes, she does."

"How many children have you?"

"Just Gilla."

"Honesty, Mr. Carmichael, is a great virtue. I want you to go home to think on what I have said today."

"And there is no possibility that I may purchase the land? For any amount?"

"No chance whatsoever. The child plans to build a home there when she is of age so that she may care for her invalid mother. A nobler child I have never met. Good day, Mr. Carmichael."

Gil pushed his way through an exit. Outside, he plunged his hands in his pockets and strode down Main Street like a fugitive. Today his last, obstinate hopes had suffered a death blow.

TWENTY-SIX

THE "FOR SALE" SIGN

With her monthly stipend, Gilla was able to buy stationery, writing pens, and stamps. She registered her address with the post office for rural mail delivery. She ordered a newspaper sent to her. The milkman came by, as well as a bread truck. With thrift, she had a few dollars left to send to her mother.

She sent Cassandra a lovely card and letter, giving her as many details of her life since their separation as possible without vilifying her father. They had differed on religion, she told her mother, and he had asked her to conform to his ideas or to leave. But God had kept her, had supplied all her needs, and now, through a miracle, she had land of her own and a tidy sum of money. Though she had been denied a college education, when she reached her majority she would be able to provide a home for both of them.

She had not seen or spoken to her father since August, she said, and he knew nothing of their chance meeting. Judo had lost his life in the war. She signed off with a promise to write every week.

Early in February, a long letter rebounded from Cassandra. She was overjoyed to hear from Gilla but was saddened to learn of Jude's death. She had hoped to meet him.

MISTER B'S LAND

She could hardly wait until she and Gilla could be together again. Did Gilla have a key to Gil's house? If so, could she get a packet of medical records from a box stored beneath the stairwell? Perhaps she could go to get them while her father was at work, Cassandra suggested.

Gilla waited for a day of sunshine when the weather was pleasant for a walk and then went to town to search for the information her mother needed. If her dad was home, she would simply tell him that she came for some records. Nothing more.

When she reached the house on Maple Street, she was puzzled. The house was vacant, a real estate sign posted in the front yard. Albriten Realty. Where had her father moved? Why had he sold his house?

She fitted the key in the door, and it opened. Inside, the rooms were stripped of furniture. Nevertheless, she found the box with the papers in the back corner of the storage space beneath the stairs. It had not been touched.

Nothing in the abandoned rooms gave her a clue to the reason for its emptiness. She locked the door behind her, her mind whirling. The abruptness of her father's decision to move disturbed her. After all, he was her father, and she would like to know if he was well or even alive. She had seen no death notice in the paper, but the dream she'd had in Amarillo flickered back to scare her.

The post office must have her father's new location listed. Gilla walked there to inquire. The postmaster told her that Mr. Carmichael left no forwarding address. Sporadically, he picked up his mail general delivery.

Gilla crossed the street to have a sandwich at a small diner. She asked the proprietor if he knew the whereabouts of her father. The man said he had not seen Mr.

THE "FOR SALE" SIGN

Carmichael for several weeks.

Next, Gilla went to the real estate office. "I came to ask about my father's house," she told the secretary. "He has it on the market—"

"Your father's house?"

"The Carmichael place."

"The big two-story brick on Maple Street?"

"Yes."

"That house now belongs to the bank."

"To the bank?"

"It was foreclosed upon. It is being sold for what is against it. Mr. Carmichael borrowed a great deal on it, and we hope to regain the amount of the loan, at least."

"Wh-where did he move?"

"I don't know, ma'am."

"The furniture—?"

"It was sold at a public auction some time ago."

"But where is my father?"

"You might check around with some of the apartment houses."

Gilla went to a public telephone and called several of the better apartments in town, but none had a Gilbert Carmichael listed.

How could she find him? What if he was ill? In need?

Gilla returned to the post office, bought a stamped envelope, and addressed it to Gil Carmichael, General Delivery. Then she dropped in a twenty-dollar bill and handed it to the postmaster.

She had done all she could do, but she returned to her cabin troubled in spirit. Why had her father borrowed so much money? What had happened that he could not repay it? He had always seemed to have plenty.

MISTER B'S LAND

What Gilla did not know is that Gil Carmichael picked up his letter before the day ended, eagerly extracted the money, and headed straight for the bar to lose it all to the demon of drink. He didn't know who sent it, nor did he care.

PAGE·A·DAY® NOTES

365 BIBLE VERSES-A-YEAR • WORKMAN PUBLISHING

6

SATURDAY · MARCH · 1999

Blessed be God, even the Father of our Lord Jesus Christ, the Father of mercies, and the God of all comfort.

II CORINTHIANS 1:3

Twenty-Seven

The Letters

Brier roses budded. Green fuzz had begun to blur the outlines of bare limbs. It was the end of March and time to plant early vegetables. Buttery sunshine warmed the crisp air.

On the sacks of seeds in the cellar, Mister B had attached seed packages that identified each species and gave the planting times. Gilla was in the garden with her hoe when her first official visitor came.

"Miss Gilla Carmichael?"

Gilla jumped and turned. The man had approached soundlessly. He was above average height with dark hair and dark brows over gray eyes. In his late twenties, Gilla guessed. His skin was weathered to a healthy red-brown, and he wore a soldier's uniform. His face was scarred.

"Yes?"

"I am David Kenworth. I was a friend of Jude Franklin—"

An inner lurch, akin to the pain of a toothache, sent weakness through Gilla's whole body, and she entertained the thought of dropping to the ground for support.

He held out a folder. "These letters were found among Jude's belongings at the headquarters barracks. I—I figured you would want them."

"Yes. Yes, I do. How did it happen? His death, I mean." She felt a scarlet flush rise to her neck and splash onto her face. She had to know.

"We were on a transport ship to Malaya when we were torpedoed. The ship sank very quickly. There was a lot of confusion. I was in the forefront of the ship, and I jumped overboard. A lifeboat rescued me. Only three of us escaped. We had burns from the explosion and were sent back to the States for treatment. The rest, our whole regiment, went into eclipse. Drowned." His words snagged on thorns of memory. "Even yet, it is hard for me to talk about."

"Thank you for telling me." It might be improper to invite the young man into her one-room cottage, the two of them alone, but Gilla wished to offer him some small courtesy. "May I bring out a stool for you and get some tea? I would like to hear more about Judo."

David stayed. "I was Jude's lieutenant," he said. "Jude was a first-class private, one of my bravest. There wasn't a speck of cowardice in him. And a finer Christian I have never met. He mentioned you many times. I almost feel that I know you." He talked for an hour, and to Gilla's hungry ears it seemed but moments.

Then he started to leave. Was it reluctantly? "It was nice to meet you, Gilla."

He was her first guest, and at once she knew that she must carry on the Brumley tradition. His legacy. "Before you go, Mr. Kenworth—"

"Please call me David." His smile softened the harshness of the scars.

"David, I have the most wonderful place to fish. My property sits with its bank to the river."

THE LETTERS

"This is your property?"
"Yes, sir. It was willed to me."
"And you live here alone?"
"Yes. Would you care to catch a fish before you go? I can guarantee you success." She gave a tight laugh. "The sand bass are running."

"Before the war, my favorite leisure was fishing," he said. "It has been two years since I have wet a hook. I would be delighted to try my hand at it again if you would go with me to show me where to cast my line."

For the rest of her life, Gilla would remember it as a special day, one of those slices of life that remain vivid and exact through the overall smudging of time gone and forgotten. She wondered if Judo might be smiling down on them. With her eyes wide open, she dreamed of him while David snagged sand bass as fast as he could keep his hook baited. There were birds' songs in the woods. The smell of earth. The first green of spring's grasses. The glimmer of the river. And her mind filled to overflowing with Judo. She had a part of him now. His letters. She must not be impolite, but she could scarcely wait for David to take his leave so that she might read them.

"Yes, Judo told me he had a sweetheart back home," David said abruptly. "He told me how lovely you were. And he didn't exaggerate."

"We were—close. We understood each other."

"You planned marriage?"

"Yes. When I grew up." Gilla laughed. "I had just turned seventeen when he left. But I've matured since then. I will be eighteen next month. I'll always love Judo even though he is gone. I think that each person may be afforded but one true love in a lifetime. Anyway, I will never marry."

"You will not want to live alone for always, lovely lady."

"Oh, I won't live alone. I will get a job and will bring my mother here with me. She lives in Amarillo and is confined to a wheelchair."

A fleeting emotion—was it disappointment?—closed over his face.

"Ah, but you are young, Gilla. Some fortunate fellow will come along and steal your heart. Setting aside your graciousness and charm, this fishing hole is enough to make me envy that man."

"No, I won't ever marry now that Judo is gone."

When David had caught a stringer of fish, Gilla offered to cook them for him. "Why, that would be grand!" he exclaimed. "I can help you. We can build a campfire to cook them right here by the river. I've done that many a time."

They chatted comfortably during their picnic. She told him how she came to inherit the place from the old man who dubbed her "Miss Joseph." After the story, he no longer called her Gilla, but she was Miss Joseph for the rest of the day.

It was late afternoon when David departed. He was kind, noble in his sacrifice for his country, but he was not like her Judo. No romantic stirrings pulled at her heart's strings. All the romance she would ever know in her lifetime died with Judo. She was sure of it.

The bundle of letters lay on the bed. She embraced them. Here was proof Judo had loved her to the end! One by one, she opened them, stopping to cry between the readings.

THE LETTERS

My Dear Gilla,
  I am not good with words and writing letters, but I am missing you dreadfully. I had hoped to see you in person before I had to ship out, to tell you how much I care for you, but you were not home. I was told that you were engaged to be married (to someone else), and I thought my heart would stop beating. But then the old man, Mr. Brumley, said that he talked with you right before you left, and you still loved me and only me.
  My own father was out of town also, and the old fellow befriended me during my short leave. I spent considerable time with him, learning and growing in God. I was saddened to find him dead that morning, but there was such a peaceful look on his face, I knew he had gone to a better world. I went to his funeral.
  I did well on my first-aid class test. I drew KP this week, and it is time to go.
                                Devotedly, JOF

Gilla folded the letter and put it on the bottom of the stack. So it was Judo who found Mister B dead. In that case, he should have been the one to find the will. In a sense, then, she had become the owner of Judo's land!

A second letter, a brief one:

Dear Gilla,
  The days drag by slowly even though we are kept very busy. I keep thinking about when this terrible war is over and I can come home to you. The whole outfit is wondering what they intend to do with us and when. But we will find out soon.
                                Love, JOF

MISTER B'S LAND

Dearest Gilla,
We just got our orders. We leave next Thursday. My lieutenant is named David Kenworth, and I really like him. We get along well. There are all kinds here. Pray for me that I can be a Christian example.
Love, JOF

My Love,
We are stationed on an island. About all we do is attend classes on Japanese intelligence and do calisthenics. A lot of the boys talk about their sweethearts back home (it keeps our minds off the present hardships). I'm glad I have a sweetheart, too. I don't say much about you except to Lt. Kenworth. He wants to meet you when the war is over.

I am not allowed to tell where we are. There are government barracks here, a headquarters where we will leave our personal belongings when we go on. There won't be any more letter writing when we go to battle. I see your beautiful face in my dreams.
Yours forever, JOF

And the last letter:

Sweetheart,
Tomorrow we sail for the last time. Tonight is my last night to write you. We will be boarding a transport before daylight. We have been told where we are going and why, but it is a top military secret. All I can tell you is that I will be riding a ship tomorrow into dangerous territory. I may not make it, dearest, but if I don't, I will count it an honor to give my life for your

freedom and the freedom of my country.
 If I survive this ghastly war, I want to spend the rest of my life with you. You can count that a proposal.
 All my love now and forever, JOF

Judo! My brave Judo! Gilla fell asleep with the letters clasped to her bosom.

Twenty-Eight

The Return

On Gilla's eighteenth birthday, her trust fund was released to her, and along with its release came an idea that seemed a command.

The exact moment of the impression's birth, Gilla could not have told. But it came with such force that she knew she must follow its bright beam. She considered no other alternative.

Build a chapel. Had the words been shouted from the sky, they could not have been more definite.

"Where, Lord?"

Here on your land.

Who would be the parson, or would it simply be a prayer chapel? Near the road? By the river?

She walked about the property, looking for a suitable location. Then she remembered the old man's wish that his land be a refuge for weary souls. A place to fish. Why not a place to fish for souls?

She knew the proper spot as soon as she found it, a small meadow that sat a stone's throw from the banks of the river, nestled among the myrtles. She would build an access road to it, put up a sign, and post a notice in the newspaper: "Haven for weary souls. Welcome." There would be a white clapboard building complete with a kneeling bench, an organ for music, Bibles, and wooden pews for those who wished to meditate. It would be open night and day. The excitement barely let her eat or sleep.

There was an urgency about the project, and she must do nothing else until it was finished. She wrote to her mother, explaining the pressing nature of her mission and promising to purchase a car and to come for her when the chapel was complete. She had to follow the call placed upon her not only for herself but for Judo, who should have been the one to claim the property, and for the old fellow himself.

Gilla wasted no time. She went to town and hired a carpenter recommended by the owner of the lumber yard. "He is the best in the county, Miss Carmichael," she was told. "And the most economical."

"How long will it take?" Gilla asked the carpenter.

"As small as the building will be," he replied, "I and my crew can have it finished by May 1."

"And the cost?"

"With a belfry, benches, pulpit, and altars—and the paint—one thousand dollars," he said. "A turn-key job."

"Can you start today?"

"I will begin first thing in the morning."

The building consumed Gilla's life, her time. She was there when the first nail was driven and hovered nearby until the workmen daubed on the last brush of paint. "Will you also make me a sign that says 'Haven for the weary'?" she asked.

"I will make it for free," the carpenter offered.

Gilla had been keyed up for a month, and the day after the chapel's completion she decided to rest, to fish, and to contemplate. It was a beautiful day, and she took a

THE RETURN

blanket to lie on the grass, enjoying the delicate harebells and rangy dandelions. Above her the sky arched, enormous, with wisps of clouds flowing through the blue. God had made a lovely world. She had no reason to feel rushed today. Nothing demanded her attention. No one would call.

If only Judo could see "his" chapel! She knew that she could have done nothing to please him more. As she sat by the river, she thought of the days past, the days to come, and the years ahead. Gone were the old possibilities of happiness, but a reason to exist sat, gleaming with white paint, on her land. Next week, she would buy an organ and would learn to play it!

Tomorrow she would post a notice of the chapel's purpose in the newspaper. Grace Chapel. That's what she would name it, with an open invitation. Who would be the first to come to her chapel for spiritual healing?

She lay on her stomach and watched as a fish leaped and scattered shards of water like crystals outlined in light. The trees stirred and swayed in the breeze. She dozed.

Then abruptly, the woods silenced. The birds aborted their songs, and the grasshoppers stopped chirping. A thump caught Gilla's attention, faint at first then becoming more distinct. What sort of animal would make a thumping sound? It sounded like a horse, striking the ground with one hoof at metered intervals. How strange!

She stood to her feet and looked about, waiting. Then she saw a man approaching, pounding a stick on the ground as he hobbled along, painfully slow. He looked harmless enough, and she had no fear. Perhaps God had sent him to her chapel. She had obeyed God's voice, and she must not be frightened of those God brought for healing.

"Gilla!" He hobbled faster. "Gilla, my love!"

Judo's voice. But it couldn't be. Judo was dead. All sense of her surroundings vanished, and nothing remained but the vague, wavering image of his face. Was this a vision? Her voice shriveled in her throat. "Judo?" she whispered.

"Yes, sweetheart. I came back to you."

"The paper said . . . David said . . . you were dead."

"I'm not." He reached for her, and she fell dazed into his waiting arms.

"Tell me, Judo—"

"When the ship broke up, I swam for as long as I could, and I resigned myself to doom when the rescue boat passed me by. They didn't see me. I prayed. Then something bumped against me, a life preserver. I clung to that for the next day and another night. The following morning, an Indonesian fishing boat spotted me and took me to the village of Java. The explosion had cut my leg somehow. I had septic shock, and I took a fever.

"I thought I was going to die of the infection, but God pulled me through. By the time I was well enough to walk, Japanese planes were coming in. I got a ride in a bullock cart to Jakarta. But the Japanese were there, and they picked me up and put me in a labor camp in Asulu.

"We had little to eat, rice and soup made of vegetable scraps. Sometimes the Indonesians threw a bit of fruit over the wire. Word got out that the Allied troops were coming to Java, so the guards abandoned us. I got a ride out with the British, and because of the condition of my leg I was discharged."

"Oh, Judo! It is too good to be true!" Gilla's tears were drops of gladness.

"I got my mustering-out pay, and I can rent us a place to live. If you assent, we will be married right away."

"We can build a house here on our land."

"You mean on your father's property among the factories?"

She grinned. "It isn't my father's property; it is mine. And there will be no factories. That is not what Mister B would have wanted for his land. I found the old man's will, which gave me everything, including the savings he left behind. And come with me, Judo." She took his hand and led him through the trees to the tiny, new chapel. "I have built this for souls who need restoring."

Judo stood for a long while looking at the chapel, awe written on his face. Then he bent to kiss her.

"We will be married in the chapel," he said.

TWENTY-NINE

THE VOICE

The jail was a stone structure behind the courthouse. Gil lay in his cell, curled up on a cot with his back to the bars. He faced a depressing gray wall, cold and shadowed. He had been booked for drunken driving. He had narrowly missed striking a pedestrian.

His license was revoked, and he could glean no money for bail. The judge who sentenced him had no sympathy for DWIs. Staring at the wall, Gil couldn't remember how long he had been here.

The whole process had been humiliating: the handcuffs, the booking, the frisking, the walk down the echoing corridor of the courthouse. Then the cold, metallic clang of the metal door closed him away from society. His dignity was battered. He no longer had confidence in the picture of himself that he had built up so painstakingly. The cell might have been a hall of mirrors in which he viewed his own image from an unexpected and repulsive angle, leaving his self-worth to collapse in shame.

The past occasionally flashed clearly, allowing him to remember his first day here. The hideous vomiting, the headache, the desperate craving for another drink. After that first day, one day merged insensibly into another, consciousness blinking on and off.

MISTER B'S LAND

When would he learn? When would he stop thinking he could conquer the world? *I was a fool,* he thought. *I have always been a fool. Did I grasp the good things in life, to cherish and to hold? No! I had to satisfy my pride. I had to prove that I could make money, could be as rich as the next fellow. And I lost everything in the process.*

Gil's own opinion of himself had been irreparably damaged. His ambitions were a sham supported by conspiracy and the exploitation of others. It had led him to this dank and dismal place, a man with many regrets, a man who had too late come to the revelation of his own foolhardiness.

He saw it now. He understood himself too well. For ten wasted years, he waited for an old man's death so that he could have his land, lusting after something that was not his, sure that it would bring his dream to reality. He'd forfeited a good job. And he had lost everything: his wife, his daughter, his home, his honor. Now he drifted, rudderless, like a wreck that didn't quite sink but was not seaworthy all the same. What had he accomplished in life? What had he ever finished?

Where had he started to go wrong? A long way back. He had abused Cassandra's sensitive nature until she could bear it no longer. Wanting her to leave, he placed the blame on her for impeding his "career." She had asked for nothing but love. She would have stuck with him through thick or thin.

Then he had tried to use his daughter as a decoy to bring game to his own dirty pond, demanding that she sacrifice her convictions, her conscience to feed his dreadful ego. He had wanted her name in the newspaper to bring glory to him. Finally, he had driven her away, a

THE VOICE

girl that any father should have been proud of. He insisted that she should conform to his own wretched lifestyle or get out. And she went. She was right, and he was wrong.

Then, to keep himself from having to face his transgressions, he drank in hopes that the tension he carried through the day would slough off. He drank in greater quantities and more often until he became an alcoholic, sunk in sloth, and rotted in loose living.

He felt miserable, heavy, dull, listless. Nothing would ever interest him again. He hated money. In pursuit of it, he had killed everything good that God had put in his life, and he had missed life's true meaning.

Well, it was water over the dam and no use drinking the same old brackish dreams. There was no one to blame but himself. He put his head in his hands and wept.

"Mr. Carmichael?"

Gil squinted his eyes to see who spoke. The jailer was unlocking the cell. "Your sentence is up today. I hope that you will shun strong drink and that I shall not see you here again."

"Yes, sir." Gil pushed himself up from the cot. Where would he go? How could he escape the nagging torment of his appetite? He could try to find Cassandra, but his driver's license had been revoked for six months. He had no idea where Gilla might be. With no home, no money, no family, and no friends, why go on with life anyway?

The jailer returned his coat to him. In the inside pocket of the coat, he had hidden a bottle of barbiturates. Today, he would use them . . . all. To end it all. It did no good to think about his sins. They just got worse.

Outside the jail, Gil made his way down the shoreline

of the river. He walked on and on until he reached the spot where he had fished a year ago, and there he dropped onto the grassy bank. Man ran through life like a rabbit with the dogs snapping at his heels. The chase always ended in death. There was no way of winning.

He opened the bottle. Suddenly, inside of him, he heard a voice. *Be silent, and sit still.*

Gil was silent and sat still, a faithless friend and husband, a despicable father. "I can't go on," he murmured.

Put away your pride.

"I need help."

Some things you must do yourself.

"It is hard."

It is hard, but you have seen yourself today. Do not sin against truth.

"What is truth?"

You will know nothing until you give yourself.

"I give myself, but I am a miserable failure."

Start over again.

"How wrong I was!"

That's better. Now you can begin. Listen!

"I'm listening."

Whosoever will come after me, let him deny himself, and take up his cross, and follow me.

"I know."

And you know that the choice is only yours?

"Yes."

Then pray.

"Oh, God," Gil prayed, "give me the strength to do this right. Show me the way."

Then he heard it, the sweet sound of music. Was he hallucinating?

THE VOICE

Determination rose within Gil. He would fight those hounds! He might not win, but he would lose with dignity! Only one sin was unforgivable, the error of giving up.

He flung the deadly drugs into the river. No, he might not win, but he would turn and fight. Those hounds would pay the price for their quarry!

He stumbled toward the music.

THIRTY

REUNION ON MISTER B'S LAND

Tomorrow was June 1, her wedding day.

Gilla, playing the organ, heard the shuffling of feet. She peeked over the big wooden instrument to see who had entered the chapel. An old man in a cloth hat and a shabby, mud-stained suit shambled in. The derelict did not raise his eyes but went directly to the altar and knelt. The chapel's first "customer." God's first assignment. A clot of emotion filled Gilla's throat.

She played on, caught up in the melodious notes of "Sweet Hour of Prayer." Wings bore her own soul to unfathomable heights of joy and thankfulness. Had anyone ever received so many blessings as she? God had let her find her precious mother, had filled her with His Spirit, had brought Judo home to her, and would bless her to be married right here in the morning.

As the broken mumbles of the kneeling man grew more urgent, Gilla played the louder, all the while praying that whoever he might be, he would find the peace he sought. That's what the chapel was all about.

Suddenly, the man lifted his head and looked toward heaven, crying out, "God, I have been an awful wretch! I am unworthy to be your child. I failed my lovely wife and my beautiful daughter. Forgive me, Father! I want nothing of this world's goods. I want only You. I am undeserving of another chance, but if Your mercy can reach me, I will take up my cross and follow You! Oh, accept the prayers of this old alcoholic. Hear Gilbert Carmichael—"

Gilbert Carmichael? What was the man saying? How did he know her father's name? The organ music stopped immediately, and Gilla stood to get a glimpse of the repenting man's face.

It was her own father! He had lost so much weight that his bones stuck out like the frame of a kite. He was gaunt, painted with wrinkles that rendered him hardly recognizable.

She flew to his side and fell on her knees beside him. "Dad!" she cried. "Oh, Dad, you have come home!" Her arms circled his shaking shoulders.

"Gilla! Oh, my little girl. Big little girl, now. You are just like your mother. Oh, can it be? Lord, is this . . . heaven? Did I die? Is my mind playing tricks on me?"

Joseph. God sent Joseph ahead to prepare a place for his father. When she had read the story the first time, God had let her know that she would be Miss Joseph; she had felt it. Now the time had come. She must finish the story of Miss Joseph. And, oh, it was so easy to forgive!

"You are still on earth, Dad. I am your daughter."

"I came here to—to the river to—take my life, Gilla. And instead, I found my life." Thin arms went around her. "Can you forgive me?"

"You are forgiven, Dad. God sent me to prepare this place for you and for others like you. I hold no bitterness. I only want you to be happy—"

"Wish not for me happiness, my daughter. I don't expect to be happy. Wish me courage and strength to

REUNION

serve my Master for the rest of my days."

Their backs were to the door, and Gilla was still holding her father's hand when other footsteps came across the threshold and up the aisle. "She is here, Thomas," a familiar voice whispered.

Gilla looked around slowly then sprang to her feet. "Mother! You are walking!"

"Yes, dear. I wanted to surprise you. But I will not disturb—" Cassandra's eyes traveled to the disheveled man at the altar.

"This is the chapel's first convert, Mother. I would like you to meet him." Her eyes held a merry twinkle.

Gil rose to his feet and turned around. "Mother, this is Gilbert Carmichael."

Cassandra teetered, clutching the end of a pew for support. "Gil?" Their eyes locked, and Gil dropped his.

"Forgive me, Cassandra. I—I could never ask you to—to take me back. Your forgiveness is all I seek."

"You don't have to ask me back, Gilbert. I am back." She smiled a tender smile. "And I have never stopped loving you. I kept believing that the real Gilbert would emerge someday."

There was a lot of catching up to do, a lot to tell and to be told. But it could wait. Gilla had an announcement to make.

"Mother, Dad, this is the happiest day of my life, but tomorrow will be even happier. For tomorrow I will wed my sweetheart and my best friend, Jude O. Franklin, and God has sent you both to make my day complete."

"Jude?" Cassandra asked. "But Jude was killed in the war—"

"Judo is very much alive, and we are very much in

MISTER B'S LAND

love. He is in town now, searching for a preacher to bind us together."

"Gil, could we—" Cassandra found Gil's eyes again, the eyes that had smitten her heart in the cotton patch, "could we renew our vows at the same time?"

Gil looked down at his dirty suit. "Like—this? I—I have nothing to offer you, Cassandra. Nothing."

"I never asked for anything but you, Gil. Remember?"

"I'll get a new suit for you, Dad," Gilla spoke. "And we will build the two of you a little house beside the river here on Mister B's land. We'll raise a big garden and—"

"Mister B's land? I thought they'd found an heir, a minor. The lawyer said—" A dawning flitted across Gil's face. "Oh, the land is yours!"

"I am only holding the property in trust for Mister B," Gilla remarked, "and he would wish nothing better for his land."

About the Author

LAJOYCE MARTIN, a minister's wife, has written for Word Aflame Publications for many years with numerous stories and books in print. She is in much demand for speaking at seminars, banquets, and camps. Her writings have touched people young and old alike all over the world.